FILIPINO
GHOST STORIES

SPINE-TINGLING TALES OF SUPERNATURAL
ENCOUNTERS AND HAUNTINGS

Alex G. Paman

TUTTLE Publishing

Tokyo | Rutland, Vermont | Singapore

Published by Tuttle Publishing, an imprint of Periplus Editions (HK) Ltd.

www.tuttlepublishing.com

Library of Congress Cataloging-in-Publication Data
Paman, Alex.
  Filipino ghost stories / Alex G. Paman. -- 1st ed.
     p. cm.
  ISBN 978-0-8048-4159-7 (pbk.)
  1. Ghosts--Philippines. I. Title.
  BF1472.P6P36 2010
  398.209599'05--dc22

                                    2010023988

ISBN 978-0-8048-4159-7

Distributed by

North America, Latin America & Europe
Tuttle Publishing
364 Innovation Drive
North Clarendon, VT 05759-9436 U.S.A.
Tel: 1 (802) 773-8930
Fax: 1 (802) 773-6993
info@tuttlepublishing.com
www.tuttlepublishing.com

Asia Pacific
Berkeley Books Pte. Ltd.
61 Tai Seng Avenue #02-12
Singapore 534167
Tel: (65) 6280-1330
Fax: (65) 6280-6290
inquiries@periplus.com.sg
www.periplus.com

Japan
Tuttle Publishing
Yaekari Building, 3rd Floor
5-4-12 Osaki, Shinagawa-ku
Tokyo 141 0032, Japan
Tel: (81) 3 5437-0171
Fax: (81) 3 5437-0755
sales@tuttle.co.jp
www.tuttle.co.jp

First edition
14 13 12 11   10 9 8 7 6 5 4 3 2 1

Table of Contents

PART TWO: Black-Out Tales from the City

PART THREE: Hauntings on American Soil

Preface

As I child, I remember dreading going down the stairs from our second-story bedroom to reach the kitchen to have dinner. The light-switch only illuminated the top of the steps, and I knew there was this dreadful, snake-haired gorgon creature that was waiting to snatch me from the shadows if my mom or siblings didn't stand at the bottom to make sure I made it down safely.

And whenever we were driven to my grandmother's house across town in San Miguel near the brewery and the Presidential Palace, my mom said that there was a giant caterpillar that lived in the water beneath a bridge that spanned the mighty Pasig River, snatching and devouring disobedient children.

I was even admonished that if I didn't eat every single grain of rice on my plate, any uneaten kernels that fell to the floor would immediately run to the Virgin Mary and report my transgression.

Worse yet, my mom warned that if I ever misbehaved if she were to pass away, she would return as a wailing ghost and grab my feet from beneath my bed if I ever let them drape down to the floor.

These were nonsensical stories, of course, meant more as teaching tools to promote good social and religious behavior, as well as a healthy and natural fear of the unknown.

But it was memories like these that would later turn my curiosity towards the supernatural. Looking back, ghost stories have seemingly always been part of my upbringing. They were told at all times of the year, day or night, at any occasion, whenever a small group of people gathered together to reminisce about the past. It was a form of oral history, taken from both my mother's and my father's sides, at a period that spanned their lifetime and ours. Whether set in the city or in the province, these stories occurred in the decades that predated cable television, the Internet, and cellular phones. These earlier times were simple, hard, but honest. Living in a third-world

Manila as seen from the province across the bay.

tropical country certainly had its challenges, but it also made one appreciate those happy occasions and the simple nuances of life.

But during the notorious rolling black-outs that seized Manila and Quezon City during the 1970s, there were plenty of reasons to be joyfully afraid of the dark. One of my earliest recollections as a child was sitting with my siblings on our balcony outside, huddled around a lit candle while trying to catch a breeze in the sweltering night air. We didn't talk about homework or the mundane events that happened during the day. Rather, we recounted the chilling ghost stories that occurred at our respective schools, or the eerie tales our relatives experienced in the countryside.

My grandparents' house in the province of Cavite, where we spent our time during summer school break, was already notoriously haunted. Local lore also held that the river right below it had a *buis*, or tax, where one person had to die there every year. There were even rumors that our house in Manila was built on a cemetery, where Filipinos who collaborated against the Japanese in World War II were singled out, executed, and then buried.

From those early times, I realized that ghost stories were commonplace not just for us, but for literally every Filipino family. Starting with the grandparents, these eerie tales often get passed on from one generation to the next, building in color and in details, until the grandchildren are hearing the same stories themselves. They were

*The foreboding river located behind the
author's old house in Naic, Cavite.*

sometimes told as a warning, as a teaching tool, for punishment, or
for just plain guilty enjoyment. Either way, it left the listener uneasy
and frightful of what was waiting for them later in the dark.

Ghostly occurrences weren't events that only happened to other
people in different blocks, cities, or countries; they were as close as
a relative's funeral.

Worse yet, these ghosts often appeared when one was alone and
far away from help. And they were usually your loved ones.

The following stories were collected from my family and from
my relatives living in the city and the province. They date back from
the early 20th century up to the late 1970s, spanning World War II,
the Ferdinand Marcos presidency, and the prosperous and tumultu-
ous times between those periods. It was a much simpler Philippines,

long gone against the shadow of today's fast-food lifestyle, and existing only in the memory of those who lived them. Just as I know nothing of my grandparents' generation, my descendants will know nothing of my own era as well.

But these short stories bridge the generations, giving a glimpse of what life was like in the past and how our ancestors existed day-to-day. Like secret food recipes, traditional ghost stories for me are valuable personal heirlooms, something to be passed forward and be proud of. It is my hope that the stories in this volume will continue to be told to future generations as a means of remembering our past.

The third section, "Hauntings on American Soil," chronicles the events that we've experienced after immigrating to the United States. In a sense, this begins a new chapter in our family history, to be explored and collected by our descendants sometime in the future.

I've had to change the names of the people involved, and embellished their background and the settings to give the reader an idea of what it was like when these stories took place.

If nothing else, this book will give readers and my family's descendants a heck of a scare, and maybe we can be remembered fondly for having kept them alive. It's been said that there's nothing

Native superstition continues to flourish, even in the shadow of progress.

in the dark that wasn't there in the light. I can only imagine who—or what—is looking over my shoulder right now as I compile these tales of the supernatural.

They've already cast their spell on me. Having heard these stories over and over, I still anticipate things to appear and stare at me from the foot of my bed, for an obscure silhouette to stand at the corner of my eye and vanish as I turn to look, or a hand to pull my leg as it inadvertently drapes over the covers to the floor.

I truly dread the day something actually does occur...

The uncharted forest best exemplifies the Philippines' link with its pre-colonial past.

Introduction

Ghosts (*multo* in Tagalog, derived from the Spanish word "muer-to," or dead), souls (*kaluluwa*), spooks (*mumu, maligno, halimaw*), and shadows (*anino*) are probably the most common supernatural entities in mainstream Filipino folklore. They are closely associated with death and the afterlife, attitudes which are largely defined by established Catholic doctrine (introduced by Spain in the 1600s), as well as by animist beliefs practiced by indigenous Filipinos centuries before that. As the only predominantly Catholic nation in all of Asia, the concepts of heaven and hell, reward and punishment, faith, prayers, and penitence are all constants in everyday life.

The centuries-old presence of the Chinese has added the Buddhist notions of karma, reincarnation, and ancestor worship to the popular consciousness, and even the geomantic art of Feng Shui has been gaining popularity in recent years. But in the southern Philippines, Islamic beliefs define concepts of the soul and of the afterlife, creating a unique cultural bridge with the neighboring Muslim nations of Malaysia and Indonesia.

Predating the arrival of the Spanish, the Chinese influence on Filipino culture continues to this day.

The mysterious balete or banyan tree, said to be the home of numerous spirits.

As much seen as they are felt, ghosts are often linked to locations where death has occurred, appearing in form from full apparitions to disembodied parts that float eerily in place. They can also manifest themselves as shadows, scents (wafting through the air like the smell of perfume or flowers), as voices that seemingly come from nowhere, or even as balls of light that travel from place to place.

Hauntings have been reported in all types of settings, again usually at the location or proximity of where a person or a group has expired. Hospital wards, old colleges, and historical monuments are common venues, as are cemeteries, previous battlefields, and even rivers and waterways. Filipino ghosts are generally solitary figures in these environments, ranging from relatives who visit their kin after burial, to seemingly malevolent souls who torment unsuspecting passersby. While some are seemingly locked in a predetermined pattern of behavior and movement, others appear to be spirits who are wandering about their grounds as if still alive.

A person's method of expiration is believed to be closely related to his or her spirit's return to the living. An extremely violent or painful death almost guarantees the spirit's return, acting as a type of spiritual residue upon the structure or location where the passing

Inside the mausoleum where the author's grandparents and great-grandparents are buried.

occurred. Deaths by suicide and by drowning are particularly feared; suicides are considered a sin in Catholicism, and drowning victims are known to seek replacement victims in order for them to move on in the afterlife.

Unfinished business is another common theme, where the spirit cannot rest until it concludes its business dealings or familial obligations when still alive. Perhaps influenced by Chinese practices, an improper burial (when a burial ritual isn't performed, or where the body is never found) is said to cause the spirit to wander. Vengeance is another motif, with the murdered person seeking revenge and divine retribution against the perpetrator.

Being touched by a ghost causes discoloration at the point of contact and can sometimes cause physical illness. These bruises usually appear in cases where a person is believed to have been pinched or "toyed with" by a ghost. Children are considered particularly vulnerable to spirits, since their immune systems are not as strong to resist them as an adult's.

Animals, particularly dogs, have long been known to be sensitive to the presence of spirits, or at least to occurrences of death. They've been observed howling spontaneously preceding mysterious events.

In mainstream Catholicism, the dead are celebrated at the end of October during All Saints Day (*Todos Los Santos,* or *Undras*), and All Souls Day (*Todos Los Difuntos*). Family members would go to the cemetery and spend the day at their loved ones' grave sites and mausoleums, cleaning and repairing them while offering prayers and lighting candles. Many even dine there, as well as spend the night. Inherited from the Spanish, this tradition parallels the Mexican *Día de Los Muertos* celebration, which is held on the same days.

Indigenous tribes practice their own unique rituals in venerating their deceased, ranging from animist customs, to Islamic rites in the predominantly Muslim south.

Communicating with spirits

The traditional way of communicating with spirits was to conduct a séance, usually with a lit candle in the middle of a table surrounded by friends or family members. Employing a Ouija Board was also a popular method, with participants taking care not to press on the shuttle too firmly to allow the spirits to move it independently.

Protection against Spirits

According to popular belief, there are three ways to protect one's self when confronted with an apparition: prayers, talismans, and preemptive blessings.

Reciting prayers when confronted with a ghost is said to drive it away. The power of holy or Latin-sounding words, together with one's faith in them, should be enough to make it disappear.

Wearing or carrying religious talismans such as rosary beads, crucifixes, and scapulars are also considered protection not just against ghosts, but anything supernatural. Mounting crucifixes on the wall, along with placing religious statues in the house, is also said to keep spirits away. Many Filipinos even hang rosary beads on the rear-view mirror of their car as added insurance to prevent injury. Possessing holy water (either blessed by a priest or procured from a holy site) is very potent against the supernatural.

Preemptive blessing simply means having a priest or a shaman ritually bless a property to drive away potentially harmful resident spirits. It is customary, for example, for Filipinos to have their homes blessed by a Catholic priest upon moving in. When residing on a new plot of land, some native Filipino tribes offer the sacrificial blood of animals upon the property (*padugo*), or fumigate it with smoke (*pausok*) prior to settling on the location.

Common Varieties

Despite the seemingly endless accounts of ghostly phenomena recorded in urban folklore, there are specific types that appear repeatedly:

Anniversary ghosts: Spirits that appear only on the date of their deaths, sometimes making their presence known by shaking or moving objects, or actually recreating their demise visually before disappearing again.

Residential ghosts: Spirits of the deceased who seemingly remain after their physical passing, usually haunting homes or locations they frequented while still alive. These can include previous home residents, and even employees of companies who either worked for a long time or perished at their jobs.

Family ghosts: Apparitions of deceased loved ones who sometimes appear at the foot of one's bed, or even in one's dreams. Though shocking to behold at first, they are generally benevolent and are considered to be only visiting the living family.

Crisis apparitions: Family-specific ghosts who make their presence known only when there is an emergency that affects their household.

Point-of-Death ghosts: Spirits that appear to loved ones seemingly at the exact moment of their passing, making their presence in a dream, as a chilling wind, or the mysterious turning of doorknobs.

White Ladies: Mysterious female apparitions dressed in white clothing, haunting specific locations at night, or appearing as hitchhikers who procure rides to reach a destination, only to disappear from the backseat upon arrival. The classic example of this is the urban legend White Lady of Balete Drive. Her profile matches the Vanishing Hitchhiker motif found worldwide.

Religious figure ghosts: Due to the Spanish influence on Filipino culture, these apparitions are described as priests and nuns who haunt churches or religious colleges. Some of the priests were said to be beheaded, a common type of execution from the country's colonial past. Nun spirits abound in all-female colleges and dormitories, as strict in the afterlife as when they were alive.

There are also occasional sightings of the Virgin Mary, and even concrete angel statues that are said to come alive and wander about at night.

Japanese ghosts: Apparitions of World War II soldiers that have stayed diligently at their post after dying, often going through their normal routine as if still alive.

Drowning victims: These souls are particularly feared, dwelling in the rivers and waterways where they perished. Because of the nature of their death, it is widely believed that these spirits seek out swimmers to drown, specifically so they can be replaced by another victim of the same fate. Besides having uncharted depths and unpredictable currents, many of the provincial rivers are infested with leeches and turn coffee-brown after a torrential rain. While growing up, we were more afraid of the river than the ocean, because we didn't know how deep it was and what exactly dwelt beneath the water.

Medical apparitions: Sightings of spectral doctors and nurses in hospitals are also common in urban folklore, either wandering the halls or riding the elevators with unsuspecting guests or patients.

Balls of fire (*bolang apoy*): Known locally as *santilmo* (or Saint Elmo's Fire), these floating orbs are said to be the souls of people who perished at sea. Another popular belief maintains that they are the restless spirits of those who were murdered, who died by accident, or were condemned to wander the earth until their sins were expiated. In some accounts, they've been known to lead people to buried treasure.

Playful elementals: Invisible, mischievous entities that toy or play tricks upon their victims. They sometimes throw rocks or spray water at unsuspecting passersby, and even tap people on the shoulder from out of thin air.

Atmospheric ghosts: Entities that mysteriously appear behind people in photographs, noticed only after the picture has been taken.

Infant or children ghosts: This is a minor class of spirits that appear in several forms. As abortion is considered a sin and frowned upon in the Philippines, the spirits of aborted fetuses are said to be sometimes heard wailing in fields. Spirit children have been known to stand on street corners and give directions to wayward drivers, only to get them even more lost. Occasionally, the ghosts of babies have been known to step on chalk and leave their footprints on blackboards of classrooms.

PART ONE

Provincial Scares

Homeward Bound

It was late at night when Mr. Tasio arrived back in his hometown. He had spent the entire day working out in the fields, rising early in the morning just to catch transportation so he could get a jump on his daily routine.

He entered the outskirts of his barrio, quietly passing the humble houses that would eventually lead to his intersection and street, and then it was off to sleep until it began all over again the following day.

Mr. Tasio was so busy staring at the bright fluorescent houselights that he was surprised to see a woman walking several dozen meters ahead of him on the dirt road. Even in the dim light and with her back turned away from him, she looked attractive; dressed skimpily with fair skin and long, black hair that was pulled to one side. She wasn't anyone he had recognized before.

He picked up his pace, walking faster to catch her attention. "Hey, wait up! What's your name? Are you from around here?"

But she kept walking forward quietly, seemingly oblivious to his calls.

As tired as he was, Mr. Tasio persisted. He could never resist a pretty girl. "What's your name? Let me catch up!"

He came closer to the woman until he was walking just behind her. Her short skirt revealed a pair of appealing legs.

The woman finally paused and sat slowly on a fallen log beside the road. Mr. Tasio approached her from behind and greeted her with enthusiasm. "What's your name?"

She slowly turned her head to stare back at him.

Mr. Tasio screamed as he found himself staring at a rotting, flesh-torn skull that was teeming with maggots.

He quickly backed away and sprinted in the opposite direction. He looked back over his shoulder and saw the woman was now pursuing him. His eyes widened into saucers when he noticed her feet weren't even touching the ground as she stepped forward in slow motion.

He ran all the way to his house and locked the door, in near-hysterics. It wasn't until the following morning that he was able to calm down and tell his story to his neighbors.

Just Below the Surface

The river behind Eric's house was always said to be haunted. Local legend held that two boys once went fishing there, just below the bridge that spanned the river. It was an innocent enough day, until something tugged on one of the boys' fishing lines. Holding on to his handmade bamboo pole, he tried to pull his catch in, but it wouldn't budge. The second boy dropped his own pole to help his friend, and both pulled on the line to drag whatever it was he caught to the shore.

But the thing beneath the murky surface was so strong that it yanked them both into the water. The boys never surfaced, and were presumably drowned.

But by what, no one exactly knew.

Soon after, rumors began to surface about their spirits living in the water, perhaps looking for victims to take their place. Even mermaids were said to be swimming about, demanding a human sacrifice.

But that didn't faze young Marco from swimming in the same spot of the river. He was a local resident who wasn't afraid of anything in the water, and was more interested in having fun than avoiding the swimming hole because of a rumor. He went with a friend to the same spot where the previous two boys were drowned, and began swimming.

He was enjoying himself immensely, until his foot rested upon something that was soft—and spongy. At first he thought it was a rock lined with underwater weeds, but he could feel hair streaming between his toes.

Marco screamed the moment he realized he was standing on the slimy head of a dead body. He quickly swam for shore, much to the surprise of his friend.

He never dared to swim in that spot below the bridge ever again. He would only stare at the water whenever he passed over, wondering what was swimming and looking back from just below the surface.

Something to Watch over me

Children who grew up in small towns in the deep province had very few options for fun in the old days. There were the occasional trips to the beach with family, or maybe to the nearby river with friends. But more times than not, it meant playing with other neighborhood children out on the street. There were no public playgrounds at that time, and the basketball courts could only be found in schools of older children some miles away.

Grace spent much of the afternoon playing tag and chasing after her friends. Their area of fun was at one of the main intersections of the town, bordering her grandmother's house, their cousin's across the street, and a rickety cement bridge that literally shook every time a truck rumbled across it. This intersection was called "Triangulo," or triangle, and was marked with a cement monument in the center of the street.

The river below the adjoining bridge was said to be haunted by the spirit of a boy who drowned mysteriously.

Grace was running with her friends back to her grandmother's house for lunch when, for some reason, she just couldn't stop herself from running faster and faster. It took tripping over a large rock to break her focus. She fell down hard on the pocked cement surface just past the bridge, bleeding and unable to get up. A passing neighbor, a friend of her grandmother who was selling sweets from a wicker basket, quickly rushed over and escorted her to her grandmother's house.

After getting cleaned up, she couldn't quite explain what happened.

"I just felt dizzy," she told her relatives. "It seemed like…something was trying to possess me, like someone wanted to get into my head."

It was the first and only time she experienced the sensation while playing near the bridge. To this day, her memories of that event remain cloudy.

A typical view in the deep coutryside. Note the Bundok na Buntis or
"Pregnant Mountain" on the right.

A View from the Top

In the Philippines, it's not unusual for relatives of all ages and generations to get together, spending time and actually bonding. Brothers and sisters, cousins and in-laws, grandparents and grandchildren often get together and share in each other's company.

Divina and her cousins did just that early one evening. They decided to play cards on the second floor of her grandmother's house in the province. She was joined by four cousins at a table, and she sat at the chair that faced the stairwell across the room that led to downstairs.

It was a nice, gentle activity to pass the time away upstairs. Divina's grandmother had a stroke, so she was unable to go up the steps anymore.

As with most houses in the Philippines, the number of steps in a stairwell is divided into threes: The first step is called "oro" or gold, the second "plata" or silver, and the third "mata" or death. Folk belief mandated that the steps must NOT end on the third count, or "mata," for it will be bad luck.

Divina and her cousins were playing a card game when they heard loud footsteps climbing up the stairwell. It wasn't anything unusual; it could've been the maid or any number of relatives who was walking up to greet them.

The footsteps were deep and pronounced, but as it paused at the stairwell's landing halfway to the top, the sound became more like creaking against the solid wood.

Everyone at the table casually turned to see who was about to meet them.

When the footsteps ended at the top of the stairs, there was nobody there.

The ghost's view of this event.

Divina's eldest cousin turned her attention back to the game and shrugged her shoulders, and everyone took her cue to just ignore it. It wasn't until years later did they discuss how unsettling that event truly was.

Mum's the Word

On those hot summer nights that Myra spent in the province during school break, she made it a habit to sleep next to her grandmother. She felt quite comfortable doing that for several reasons: they slept inside the protection of a mosquito net, her grandmother kept her cool with her hand fan, plus the fact that they were both women. Her grandfather had been dead for years, so Myra kept her grandmother company.

Even at night, the sweltering heat of the tropics could be hard to bear, so the locals kept themselves cool as best they could. It couldn't always be raining (when the air was much cooler) or even winter time where the temperature drops for several balmy and acceptable months.

Myra also had this other habit of burying her head just between her grandmother's shoulder blades when her back was turned in the opposite direction. It somehow made her feel more secure.

She woke up one evening, and found the air to be unusually cold. There was really no reason for it to be freezing, considering it was still summertime.

▼ *Provincial life is best defined by the vast rice fields that sustain it.*

But then she heard her grandmother talking to someone, and what she said brought chills down her young spine.

"What are you still doing here?" asked her grandmother to someone in the pitch blackness. "The little one might get scared."

Was she talking to her deceased husband? Myra sealed her eyes shut and pretended to be still sleeping, not bothering to ask the following morning who her grandmother was really talking to.

Not Amused

Bobby kept a secret that he didn't know how to explain to his grandmother: he had filed papers to finally immigrate to America. He wasn't sure, however, how she would take the news, given that she much preferred for him to stay at home and watch over the family.

He slept at her place one night, in the middle bedroom on the second floor, whose main window faced a lit bridge behind the house. He didn't need a mosquito net, because he had just manually pumped the room with bug spray.

Bobby woke up in the middle of the night and rubbed his eyes. With light seeping in through his window from the bridge outside, he suddenly saw his deceased, silver-haired grandfather standing at the foot of his bed, dressed in his burial clothes of a *Barong Tagalog* (native formal shirt) and black pants.

His grandfather's face was expressionless, and he had his hand on the railing of Bobby's bed.

Bobby didn't want to blink at first. Local belief held that if a person blinked while seeing an apparition, the apparition would disappear. But he blinked out of fear anyway, and his grandfather still stood there looking on.

He must not have been happy with Bobby's secret of leaving for America.

Grabbing his pillow and blanket, Bobby leapt from his bed and bolted out of the room. Reaching the stairwell that led to downstairs, he grabbed the banister and swung himself around to take one final glance behind him.

His grandfather had let go of his bed's railing and turned to face him fully, still expressionless.

Bobby went straight to his grandmother's room downstairs, jumping over her and squeezing himself between her body and the wall.

When she asked what he was running from, he said he would just tell her the following morning.

On Dark and Stormy Nights...

It wasn't unusual for Janice's grandmother to be sitting out on her porch at night. Janice lived just across the street, so she was used to seeing her out front nightly from her window.

Her grandmother's family owned a sprawling rice processing mill, and the main house was flanked by a granary on one side, and a towering mound of rice husks that bordered a river behind it. They also kept a stable of pigs in the rear, fed by the rice husks and accessible only through wooden stairs.

This mound of husks had already been rumored to be haunted by a headless Spanish priest, who was said to walk on top of its surface at night without disturbing the grains.

One rainy night, Janice saw a figure covered in a white dress from head to toe descend down the stairs to the rear of the house, near

The main church in the author's municipality, the spiritual center of the community.

the rice husk mound and the pigpen in the back. She assumed it was her grandmother, but wasn't sure why she would go to the back at all, especially in the dark. Was she going there to pee?

From her window, she decided to stand guard and wait for her to come back up. But when her grandmother didn't return after a long while, Janice got tired and decided to go to sleep.

The following morning, she saw her grandmother and asked her what happened.

"Why did you go downstairs to the back when it was so dark?" she asked. "I was waiting for you to come back up. What took you so long?"

"Oh," she replied calmly, "that wasn't me. You saw the White Lady. She shows herself whenever it rains."

Tonight's Fare

Like the iconic jeepney, Filipino tricycles are a common mode of transportation throughout the country. Best described as a heavily-

The town's tricycle station, its lifeblood of transportation.

decorated motorcycle with a roofed sidecar, it can be found in both rural and urban settings, meant as a cheap and convenient alternative to distances that are too far to walk but not so far as needing a car. Filling the sidecar with passengers can be challenging, sometimes reverting to seating the extra passenger just behind the driver.

Mr. Gus was one such driver, either waiting at the tricycle station, or doing his rounds around the neighborhood to pick up needy passengers.

Fares came in less and less as the evening progressed, usually as the daily night market began closing down. But needing extra cash, he decided to circle his barrio one more time for a chance passenger.

He saw a woman in the distance, nearly obscure against the dim houses behind her, and waving her arms to catch his attention.

Mr. Gus promptly drove up and parked his tricycle in front of her.

"Where are we going?" he asked, routinely.

"On the other side of town," she said. "Just go and I will tell you where to turn."

He glanced at her casually from the corner of his eye as they drove off, noticing she was dressed all in black. "You're out a little late," he said, raising his voice above the loud engine.

She kept her gaze forward and didn't respond.

He had driven her to the far side of town, but still wasn't sure where they were going.

"Where did you say you lived again?" he asked.

"Just follow the road. I will tell you where to turn."

They reached the outskirts of town, with little lighting and even less houses to guide by. His patience was wearing thin.

"Here," she finally said, pointing to a dim house virtually in the middle of nowhere. "I live here."

Mr. Gus parked his tricyle to the side of the road and left it idling as the woman exited the sidecar.

"That will be ten pesos," he said with a forced smile. He thought of charging her extra for making him drive to seemingly nowhere.

The woman extended her hand and produced two coins, but then the coins mysteriously flew out of her palms and struck him in his eyes.

Recovering quickly—if painfully—he squinted his eyes to stare at the woman who apparently tried to blind him.

But she disappeared, and there were no structures around where she could've hidden.

Mr. Gus nervously drove away and didn't bother to look back, frightened at who—or what—his fare truly was.

Wait and See

Willy had a reputation for being fearless in his barrio. An avid hunter and marksman, he always carried a gun with him wherever he went and never backed down from anything.

One stormy night, when his parents had traveled to the big city, Willy decided to spend time with relatives who lived across the street from his house. The rain was particularly torrential, causing the nearby street lamp to flicker, and with lightning forking all around them.

As he was exchanging stories with his aunts and uncles, he happened to glance at his house across the road and saw a mysterious light floating on the second floor. It was almost as if someone was walking its length, going from room to room, while holding a candle.

Willy immediately thought it was a thief rummaging through his house.

"Ignore it," admonished his elders. "Just pray."

"But it could be someone stealing from the house," he protested. He wanted to go over and confront whoever it was.

"Don't go in the house," they persisted. "It might be a soul that got lost and just wants to appear to someone to greet them, or to say goodbye."

Willy looked on as the mysterious light vanished at the top of the stairwell.

"Just sleep at our house," his aunt said. "Go back there in the morning."

Willy returned to his house with a cousin the following day, still thinking it may have been a thief. But when he checked the front door, it was still locked. Upon entering and searching the second floor, nothing was touched or stolen.

He never forgot what he saw that fateful night.

The Creek

It was May, a full month before the beginning of rainy season. Ernesto and his friends wanted to go fishing the next day, but they didn't have any bait. He decided to go to the creek alone the night before and catch some frogs.

He left his house around 11:30 in the evening, bringing a flashlight and a .22 caliber automatic pistol for the snakes he might encounter along the way. The creek itself was about a third of a kilometer from his home, and his neighbors admonished him for going alone at night.

"No problem," he said. He knew the town and its people by heart, so he wasn't really afraid of anything he might encounter. Wearing his wide brimmed, Mexican-style hat, he went off to find some frogs.

He arrived at the creek and began searching, going as far as wading in the rice paddies. But to his surprise, there were no frogs to be found.

In-between towns one finds nothing more than vast fields,

That was when he felt something splatter against his hat. He looked down and saw the water ripple around him. Someone was tossing sand from a distance. When another spray struck his hat again, he realized someone was trying to scare him.

Ernesto pulled out his gun and fired three shots in the air. It was his turn to put the scare on the prankster.

"Who's doing this?" he said. "I want to talk to you."

But there was just dead silence.

He then asked the same question in Spanish. There were rumors that the ghost of a Spaniard was wandering the area, and he wanted to know if it was that ghost.

When no one answered, he then spoke in English, and then back to his native Tagalog. Because he held a gun, Ernesto expected someone to get scared enough to come out and plead for mercy.

But there was only silence around him. Not finding anymore frogs, he decided to call it a night. When he arrived back home, he then discovered some sand inside his shirt pocket. It would've been impossible to have come from the splatter earlier, because of his wide-brimmed hat.

winding waterways, and bordering forests.

Ernesto took the sand as a sign not to come back. Although he wasn't afraid, he respected it enough to honor the warning.

Reconnected

Richard's mother was on the phone when he arrived home from school. His family had immigrated to America from the Philippines two decades before, and the only contact he received from relatives came in the form of handwritten letters, or long-distance phone calls that came in the middle of the night, as there is a 16-hour time difference between both countries.

He waited for his mother to finish her conversation before greeting her with a hug.

"Who were you talking to, mom?" he asked.

"Your cousins in the province," she said. "They're saying that one of your relatives is haunting their old home."

Richard gave her a puzzled look. "What do you mean?"

"Cousin Rey said that one of our relatives became very ill at your Aunt Gladys's home. Your Aunt Gladys has been dead for several years. The maids are now saying they've seen her in the house at night."

He smiled. "You're not serious…"

"Oh, yes," she said. "The maids have seen her blouse floating up and down the hallway with nobody inside it. They've also seen your aunt with just her upper body, with no legs."

"And this started because someone in the house got sick?" he asked.

"Some ghosts are just that way," she said matter-of-factly. "They show up to make their presence felt only when there's a family emergency."

Richard was planning on taking a vacation back in the Philippines to get reconnected with his culture. Prior to his mom's conversation, she suggested that he stay in his Aunt Gladys's old house to get reacquainted with relatives.

Postcard from the Past

Rosa and her younger brother Arsenio grew up during the Japanese occupation of the Philippines during World War II. During that period, many Filipinos devised secret, non-verbal ways of communicating with each other without being detected.

Despite advances in technology, most barrios still keep their secrets to themselves.

After the war, Arsenio would later become a professor at a prestigious university in Manila. He would also sire twenty children from two different women.

When he retired, he moved back in with his older sister Rosa.

He also had this habit of placing a leaf on top of his sister's mosquito net while she slept, a remnant from their upbringing, and signifying that he had left the house to go into town. She would immediately know where he was upon waking without having to ask. These protective nets were an absolute necessity in the province, to protect against mosquitoes that fed at night.

But he died before she did, and life went on.

Rosa woke up one morning, months after his death, and much to her surprise, she saw a single leaf placed on top of her mosquito net, signifying that her deceased younger brother had left to go to town.

The Bridge

"Tulay na Malamig," literally "The Cold Bridge" in Tagalog, was a bridge on the outskirts of town that connected two adjoining barrios. It was also a structure that many people were quite afraid of due to its history: Three bodies were said to have been dumped over its railing after a well-publicized massacre had taken place at the adjacent barrio. A mayor, a chief of police, and a policeman were said to be the victims.

Locals also told of seeing a mysterious female apparition, a floating disembodied head, haunting the bridge at night near the bamboo thickets that bordered its edges.

But in truth, this "ghost" was a living woman who was just expressing her grief.

Helena was heartbroken when she lost her elder son, a doctor, to tuberculosis. But during his funeral, she didn't cry a single tear or express any emotions, bottling up her feelings deep inside.

At night, however, she found a way to express her grief the only way she knew how. Dressing up in black with a shawl over her head, she went to the Cold Bridge while smoking her cigar and began gathering firewood.

Collecting wood near the bridge made sense to her, because below it was the river, and that was where the wood grew from.

But her countenance, lit only by the cigar's smoldering embers beneath a black shawl, must've been a terrifying sight for unwitting passersby, who were to too afraid to approach her nightly by the roadside.

Thus was the legend born of the "ghost" that haunted the "Tulay na Malamig." It was a broken-hearted mother grieving for her son.

She had to Go

Rowena and her family decided to open up a restaurant on the bottom floor of a two-story, Spanish-style building. Situated just across the street from a popular bowling alley and adjacent to a store that sold shoes, it was an ideal location to draw hungry customers, even at night.

But the building itself already had a reputation prior to Rowena's arrival. Not only was it the past home of a famous national song-

Religious fiestas abound in the province.

writer, the restaurant's waitresses who lived on the second floor also reported experiencing "unusual" events. Light switches turned on and off for no reason, and the staff even heard mysterious footsteps coming from the fragile rain gutters that encircled the roof. Rowena herself called the police to investigate, but nothing—or no one— was ever found.

One night, just as the restaurant was about to close, the cook and the waitresses noticed a woman walk through the front door and go inside the restroom. The workers thought nothing of it, preoccupied with cleaning the tables and filling up the kitchen's water supply for use the next day.

But the woman remained inside the restroom for an unusually long time, and one of the waitresses needed to relieve herself.

"Hoy," she said, knocking on the door. "What's taking so long in there? We're closing, and I have to use the restroom, too."

The door opened by itself. When the waitress peeked inside, there was nobody in the room. It was virtually impossible for the woman to have exited the room without being noticed by the workers, and the restroom itself had no windows.

Hide and Seek

Angel knew someone was stealing her family's chickens and eggs. They kept a sprawling poultry enclosure behind their house, and some of the birds and their young began disappearing by morning.

One night, she decided to stand guard from inside her house to see if she could catch the perpetrator in the act. With her husband's .22 caliber rifle in hand, she was going to fire into the air and scare anyone she saw stealing. But as she peered out of her venetian-style window, she frighteningly saw a tall, dark shadow run to the back of her property, behind a large caimito tree. Caimito is a tropical fruit known also as a star apple, describing the unusual asterisk design dividing its flesh inside.

Waking her husband and helpers, she instructed one maid to run to the police outpost situated at the street corner and get help. Angel and her husband, the helpers, and three policemen approached the tree from three directions: from the house, the street, and the garage entrance. Even their dogs were wailing, as if sensing something un-natural was in the backyard.

But when they arrived at the caimito tree where they thought the thief was hiding, there was nobody there.

"Whatever you saw wasn't human," remarked one policeman. "It was probably a ghost that just likes to show itself."

Angel learned her lesson about looking out her window at night, and vowed never to do it again.

Great balls of Fire

According to Grandmother Elena, seeing fireballs at night was once common in her block. She would watch one soar through the air behind her neighbor's house across the street, floating between the property and the river. These fireballs were also believed to lead peo-ple to treasure, particularly riches that wanted to be discovered. However, whatever treasure was hidden beneath the ground must be dug up immediately after the fireball's impact, otherwise it would turn to dust.

When Grandmother Elena was younger, a fireball did land near her family's fishpond by her house. Initially fearful of the event, the men in her family decided to wait until the following morning to see what lay beneath the impact crater. In the daylight, they unearthed Spanish-style tiles and bricks that were formed into a hollow cone.

But the cone was empty, except for ashes that filled its center.

They waited too late to retrieve the treasure.

Our House

When Reyna was young, she and her family lived in a sprawling, two-story house next to the town market in their barrio. It was an unusually tall property, formerly belonging to a Spanish family, with wide floors where she and her friends would play an old game called "hihip." Lying on one's stomach, each player would try to blow two rubber bands on top of the opponent's simply by using one's breath, and the first one to do so was the winner.

Unfortunately, the house was also notorious for the number of people who died there before. Reyna and her family experienced their share of "unusual" activities while living within its walls.

They would regularly hear footsteps in the attic, heavy steps as if made by someone wearing boots. Her grandfather went up the one entrance to the attic, which was located inside a bedroom, and

In the searing summer heat, time seems to stop in the countryside.

saw no one there. He later installed a light bulb inside the room, in case he needed to enter again.

While in the hallway, her seven year-old cousin saw a small figure emerge from the ornate carvings that capped the tall windows beneath the ceiling. He described it as a "duwende," or dwarf.

Even with all the capiz shell windows closed and no leaks from the attic, something would douse family members with a cupful of water while sitting inside their rooms.

In the bathroom, they would hear water running, as if someone was taking a shower, when there was nobody inside.

Her aunt was even hit with a pillow, from something that seemed to have rolled it across the floor like a bowling ball.

Although the house was turned into a hospital years after they moved out, Reyna and her family still recall their experiences there with a sense of fear and wonder.

Grandma

Up until her passing, Nora's grandmother Letty lived with her and her family in the same household. But even in death, she continued to make her presence felt to those who remained behind, going about her chores, and even expressing her displeasure.

Nora and her family were watching television one night in the living room. The room was flanked by a small bar from behind, and had a single, shaded lamp on its counter. Earlier in the day, Nora had spanked her son Tony as punishment, someone whom her deceased grandmother was quite fond of. As they were enjoying the show, the lamp suddenly began to flicker in place.

"Ala!" mocked Nora's relatives, "Grandmother Letty is not happy you spanked Tony."

On another occasion, the family was again watching television. In those days, it was customary for Filipino families to wrap their furniture in plastic, to prevent them from getting dusty or soiled. They had two couches in their living room, one in front and one in the back, and the rear one was unoccupied.

As they were watching, they were surprised to hear the plastic from the rear sofa creaking loudly, as if a person suddenly sat down and put weight on its surface. They turned around, and saw nobody there.

Where the author's family used to star-gaze at night.

One of the relatives that stayed at Nora's house was Rodrigo, a well-respected lawyer who was not prone to believing folk superstitions or ghost stories. While Nora was playing bingo with her aunt in the alley just outside their house, Rodrigo decided to take a bath in the second-story bathroom. As he was drying himself, he suddenly heard the distinct sound of sweeping against the bathroom door and on the floor, made by a flexible palm frond broom used commonly in provincial households.

Nervous, he went to another room and peered out the window that overlooked the bingo game playing in the alley.

"Did someone come up here?" he asked. "I heard someone sweeping against the door."

"No," said Nora. "That must be Grandmother Letty."

There were also other unnatural events that happened in her home. A female student who was staying with Nora as a border to get through school was once assigned to retrieve rice, which was kept in a container in the rear of the living room. As she bent down to scoop, an aluminum ash tray suddenly flew forward and struck her. She quickly ran upstairs in a panic.

Grandmother Letty also owned a cabinet that was supposedly always locked. Yet after she passed away, Nora and her family would sometimes see its drawers pulled open when they walked by, and no one had access to the key.

Nora and her family have since left the house and immigrated to America. She heard word that once the property was vacant, people reported seeing a so-called "white lady" peering out into the street from the windows.

Catch of the Day

The river that ran below the barrio's most haunted house shared the same reputation as the structure that towered above it. People for generations had always reported unusual activity occurring in both locations, ranging from toilets being heard flushing by themselves when the property was unoccupied, to the curious smell of garlic being fried alongside the lone river below it.

But that didn't stop a man from fishing its shores for shrimp one day. Freshwater shrimp and crabs were commonplace foods in the province, easily caught and quite bountiful. This man owned a net that was woven between two bamboo poles, which were crossed over each other like a letter "x." Resting these poles on the river-bottom ahead of him, he would then scoop up whatever prey the currents brought inside it, storing the catch inside a woven fish basket tied around his waist.

The author's old house in the province, home to many of his family's ghost stories.

As he was wading waist-deep in the water, the river unexpectedly began to swell. He immediately extended his net forward to catch whatever was in the currents, then grabbed it at its fulcrum to raise it up. To his surprise, he saw a large amount of shrimp, crabs, and mudfish trapped inside his net.

He repeated the technique several times, astonished at the bounty he was catching. However, as he raised his net one time to sort out the catch to be placed inside his basket, he saw something unusual among the shrimp and crabs.

A disembodied hand and forearm was groping inside his net.

Were his eyes playing tricks on him? This ghostly hand was grabbing at the shrimp and crabs alongside his own. It would lift up what it caught, vanish, then reappear inside the net and resume grasping for more.

The fisherman ignored it at first, only half-believing what he saw. His harvest from the river continued to grow bountifully, seemingly as long as the hand was there.

But he eventually grew irritated; why should he share his catch with this greedy apparition? His commonsense finally got the better of him as he realized that he was trying to compete against a ghost.

Frightened, he quickly waded back to shore.

Next-Day Heir

While Grandmother Lucia lay on her deathbed, speculation was already rampant among her family and relatives. She was said to be the possessor of a talisman that gave her the power to disappear at will, and per folk belief, she had to pass it on to a successor before she could die. It was what was keeping her alive.

In her younger years at the turn of the century, she and her husband were revolutionaries, part of a band of rebels in a historic barrio who opposed any foreign occupation of the Philippines during the Spanish-American War.

When her family's position was revealed to the Americans by a local spy, her husband was shot in the leg while trying to retrieve his horse to escape. He was captured and sent to a field hospital. His severe wounds later led to his leg getting amputated. When he awoke and found himself in the company of Americans, he resisted, jumping up and down and refusing to live under the banner of a foreign nation. His wound hemorrhaged, and he would later die from his injuries.

Lucia replaced her husband in the group, dressing herself up as a man and continuing their plight against American rule. She even exacted revenge on the traitor that led to her husband's capture and death.

But old age and cirrhosis of the liver had caught up with her in her later years, and no one knew who she was going to pass the magical amulet on to.

Grandmother Lucia instructed all of her children to leave the room, but one of her daughters initially refused to, fearful that her mother was going "to elope," a euphemism for dying alone. She eventually relented and walked outside to the patio. The helpers told the children to remain quiet, lest the talisman lose its potency. They turned off the lights in Grandmother Lucia's room and left her alone.

As this daughter was waiting out front, she suddenly heard the sound of coins dropping to the floor, tinkling as they hit the ground. That was when she knew her mother had finally released the talisman from her body.

Grandmother Lucia passed away in peace the following morning, and to this day, no one knows who possesses her valued talisman.

Tag, You're "It"

Donny was just a face in the crowd, one of thousands of children in the barrio who went to elementary school by day, then played with his friends soon afterwards. Aside from watching television inside a relative's house or swimming at the beach or river, there really wasn't that much to do in his small municipality, except perhaps playing around the forest trails or rice fields to look for anything curious to see.

Enduring a particularly hot and boring school day, upon getting home Donny quickly changed from his uniform and joined some friends out in the nearby glade, which was located a short distance behind his house.

Finding a clearing, the group began chasing each other in an impromptu game of tag, tapping each other alternately while running full-speed until they were out of breath. But while evading his classmates, Donny suddenly lost his footing and fell on the soil, falling down awkwardly with a painful wince.

"Are you alright?" his friends asked, collectively running forward.

He raised his elbow, then dusted off the moist stain that covered his left side. "I'm fine. I just tripped."

They played a while longer before deciding to call it a day. Donny wasn't too worried about his mishap; he was playing in old clothes, and he didn't hurt himself too badly.

But that night, something didn't feel right, particularly his leg. Between the time he finished his chores and brushed his teeth, he found himself limping curiously to bed.

At school the following day, he waddled about awkwardly while going from class to class, dragging his right leg as if it was longer than his left. Donny explained his condition to friends as stemming from his fall from the previous day, and that he would get better soon. But he couldn't hide his condition from his mother, who immediately saw his stride as soon as he came home.

"Why are you walking that way?" she asked with concern. "What's wrong with your leg?"

Only the towering palm trees truly see what goes on after dark.

"I just fell," he said. "I'll be okay."

But his condition persisted even after a few days. His mother stared at how Donny continued to drag his right leg as if it was literally longer than the other. She even wondered if it could be the onset of polio. One night, she approached him while he was asleep and measured both his legs from hip to toe, to see if there was a discrepancy in length.

They were still equally the same.

Unable to stand her son's suffering any longer, she brought him to a *mangtatawas* (or folk doctor) to have him diagnosed. Unlike traditional doctors, the folk doctor also specialized in illnesses that stemmed from supernatural causes.

The folk doctor dripped hot wax from a lit candle into a glass jar of water, and then carefully observed the patterns floating on the surface. Performing other rituals, he then gave them his diagnosis.

"Something is clinging to your son's leg," he said ominously.

"Donny fell down while playing out in the glade," she explained to the doctor, "and that's when everything began."

"When he fell," he ascertained, "he must've disturbed someone—or something—that lived there."

The belief that mysterious spirits lived in remote areas was quite common in the province, so this unnerving news wasn't a complete surprise.

"Burn leaves and incense at the very spot where he fell," recommended the folk doctor, "as a peace offering."

Donny's mother did just that, arriving at the very spot the next day and covered it with billowing smoke.

That very night, Donny's leg felt normal again, and he stopped limping.

Something on my Mind

Unlike their prolific siblings and relatives who continued to add to their clan's numbers, married couple Cathy and Dean produced only a single child. But it was a happy household, simple to maintain, and their child Alvin was a model son. He followed his parents' orders obediently and didn't get into trouble while in elementary school.

And that was why Dean would quickly notice if anything was

amiss about his boy. One morning, as his son joined him and his wife at the breakfast table, Dean noted something different about his son's appearance: his hairline seemed to be receding.

It must've been the light, the father thought to himself. How could his boy be losing his hair at such a young age? His normal routine was just going to school, heading home, playing, and then retiring to his room after dinner to sleep. Alvin did spend a lot of time in his room, but Dean never really saw that as anything out of the ordinary.

Dean also reasoned that the boy simply may have inherited his bloodline's unusually high forehead, a curious remnant from their Spanish ancestry.

But as weeks went by, Alvin's hairline continued to recede further, almost as if the hairs were being plucked intentionally.

Unable to come up with a reasonable explanation, Cathy and Dean decided to sit Alvin down to find out for themselves what was really going on.

"Son," said Dean calmly, "you are losing hair at the front of your head. Is someone doing this intentionally? Is someone picking on you in school?"

"I'm the one doing it, dad," Alvin said resolutely. "I'm pulling my own hair out while inside my room."

"But why?" asked Cathy in shock.

"Because of the little boy," replied Alvin, frustration building in his voice.

Dean stared at him in disbelief. "What little boy? You live in your room by yourself…"

"The little boy in the corner that no one else can see," said Alvin, already groping for his scalp. "He's been getting on my nerves so much lately that I've been ripping my hair out in frustration."

Caught in the Wake

Drownings in the river were an unfortunate reality in the province. Whether pulled under by the unpredictable currents, or carried away in the swollen, coffee-brown waves of the rainy season, lives lost in the water had always carried with them a stigma of rumor and of mystery.

No one really knows what lurks beneath the countryside's waterways.

Jeffrey was a popular boy from a wealthy family that owned a thriving business. As was the case with having successful parents, his family was constantly linked to local intrigue—and to tragedy.

One warm day, he and several of his friends decided to go to a popular swimming hole and have fun. But to his friends' horror, Jeffrey drowned right before their eyes.

Rumors spread like wildfire in the small barrio when the news got out. Not only did the details of his death come into question, but also the character of the friends he swam with, as well as the various controversies his entire family had long been linked to. Where exactly were his friends at the time of his drowning, and why didn't they try to rescue him? Was his death also a form of divine punishment for all the infidelity and the corrupt business dealings his parents were long rumored to be part of?

Lost among the wild speculation was the grief that Jeffrey's family endured, particularly his two younger siblings who now had to face the death of an older brother.

But even more disturbing were the comments that the policemen made after retrieving the young boy's body from the water.

It was definitely Jeffrey who drowned, but there was something different about his face. Something on it had changed.

According to the policemen, it was almost as if someone—or something—had played with his facial features and rearranged them.

They speculated that enchanted spirits in the water may have taken fancy to his body prior to it being recovered.

When Visiting Hours are Over

Aster and her nine siblings faced perhaps the most tragic scenario any family could face: both their parents died within the same year, their mom passing away on Christmas Eve. With no relatives wanting to support them, and their parents insisting prior to their passing that they be not given away individually to separate families, the children were left to their own devices to survive.

It was up to the eldest brother to make sure his siblings were fed daily, even if it meant eating just one square meal a day. The youngest member was only seven months old at the time.

The children lived in a two-story house with an old woman, who charitably looked after them. They slept inside one mosquito net in the living room at night, with the rest of the house remaining empty. They often wore red-colored clothing while sleeping, stemming from a folk belief that the spirits of dead parents would not visit their living children if they wore red, perhaps because it resembled the shade of hellfire.

Against their daily adversity, there was one event that they just couldn't overcome: the youngest sister just wouldn't stop crying.

The siblings couldn't understand why she continued to weep for no apparent reason, day and night.

Finally, their caretaker had had enough. She took a pillow and stormed upstairs, opening the door to one of the empty bedrooms. She threw the pillow inside and began to lecture at whoever was inside with unrestrained anger.

"Okay, here is your daughter!" she shouted. "I keep trying to comfort and help your children, but you keep visiting them! I am leaving them now!"

The very next day, the youngest child stopped weeping, and the caretaker returned. She theorized that the seven-month old kept crying, because her deceased parents kept visiting her, reminding her constantly of their demise.

Signs

Along with folk healers who used prayers and massage to treat patients of various ailments, fortune-tellers who used palmistry and numerology were also quite common in the deep province. These skills were often passed on from elders, learned intuitively, or were actually foreign-based methods that had been imitated and then re-christened in the local language as being traditional.

Laarni initially hesitated to accept the statue of the Santo Niño (or Baby Jesus) when it was offered to her by the previous family who borrowed it. There was a tradition in her church that involved passing around the sacred statue between households in the community for a period of seven days. This brief time of possession usually involved prayers, singing, and communal veneration among neighbors wishing to come and worship.

Despite the amount of work that went into hosting and feeding visiting parishioners for a full week, she ultimately acquiesced and decided to do it for the sake of the community.

On the first day of the celebration, Laarni learned that a fortune-teller of Vietnamese descent was also going to visit the Baby Jesus statue in her home. She became curious as to what this person, whose skills were already well-known among fellow church-goers, would reveal to her.

But she was also quite shy, so she invited three in-laws to be by her side while she requested a personal reading.

Sunset in the province, where the night is so dark that it is almost impossible to distinguish the sky from the horizon.

"Did you lose both your parents a long time ago, when you were very young?" asked the woman eerily.

"Yes," responded Laarni, shocked at her very first question.

"Don't worry," reassured the fortune-teller. "They're still here."

Laarni didn't know what to say. She did indeed lose parents, just as the woman described, and she and her siblings struggled greatly early on just to survive.

"They stayed, because they love you," the fortune-teller said. "The next time you are cooking rice, raise a cupful in your hands and dedicate it to them. This will show that you still remember them, as well."

Will the Real Haunted House Please Stand Up?

Napoleon lay quietly on his bed and stared at the trappings of the guest room. It had been over twenty years since he returned home to the Philippines after immigrating to America with his family at a very young age. This was his first trip back as an adult, and so much had changed that he could barely recognize the barrio he once called home.

His many relatives were kind enough to give him lodging, taking turns showing him around while letting him stay in their homes. Napoleon barely knew these people, but they sure knew his father, and it was this familiarity and familial debt that afforded him this vacation.

His current lodging belonged to a lawyer who was helping his family deal with legal issues stemming from property his father owned. This lawyer was also a distant relative, and allowing Napoleon to stay there also allowed him to become a courier of sorts for important documents that needed to be exchanged between the two families.

But Napoleon's immediate concern wasn't about the peripheral business of his parents, but rather about having a good time. Unfortunately, there was one nagging concern that prevented him from having a single peaceful night's sleep.

One of the houses where he was scheduled to stay was supposedly haunted.

He didn't know which one it was, and neither did his parents, even though they were the ones who first broke that news to him. All of his relatives' names blended together into simply "aunt" or "uncle," and he couldn't tell one person's informal nickname from another.

Napoleon had stayed in two previous locations prior to his arrival at the lawyer's house, and they were all uneventful at night. Beyond the opaque mosquito nets that cocooned his bed and the Catholic idols and Chinese furniture that decorated those houses, all was peaceful.

His current lodging may very well had been the haunted home he was dreading. And in case it was, he was keeping the lights on all evening long. He didn't want to be caught off-guard should something mysteriously appear at the foot of his bed.

Napoleon woke up in the middle of the night and turned to the window adjacent to his bed. He heard a choral hiss emanating from behind the curtain that covered it, and deduced that it was raining outside. It was June, after all, the start of wet season.

When he sat up to close the window panes shut to prevent water from leaking in, he quickly saw it wasn't water sizzling outside the screen frame.

It was hundreds of winged, flying ants.

They were drawn to his bedroom light and were slowly seeping in through the window frame's misaligned corners.

Napoleon stared in disbelief as they formed a small cloud before him and began alighting on his bed. He quickly grabbed his heavy suitcase and wheeled it into the hallway, turning off the lights as he shut the door behind him.

With no light source to be drawn to, he figured that the ants would just go away. He casually walked to the bathroom at the end of the hallway to urinate. But the moment he flicked the lights on, a familiar hissing sound grew against his window.

The insects had followed him and the light, turning the corner around the house to congregate again in droves.

Napoleon had had enough. He made sure his suitcase was zipped shut and intact before going downstairs quietly, lying down on the sofa with the lights off. He didn't want to bother his relative with his encounter, so he endured the clicking geckoes and ravenous mosquitoes and went to sleep.

Many isolated communities exist between uncharted roads and the forest.

He was awakened at sunrise by a hired maid, who came to the house everyday to do chores. He later told his relative what had happened over breakfast, and it was dismissed as a typical experience in the deep province.

Napoleon later returned to his room and saw that the ants had all but disappeared, except for a large, bulb-headed queen that was crawling on his bed. He then went outside and took a stroll in the backyard, and found two mounds of fragile, glittering wings piled neatly on the ground.

The ants had mysteriously vanished in the sunlight.

He left the house the following day without incident, and was later told that the haunted house he was dreading was actually the very first home he stayed at in the province, not the lawyer's.

That must've been why he shared the room with an elderly uncle during his initial stay there, and why an opaque mosquito net surrounded his bed while he slept: so he couldn't see what stood outside of it in the dark.

Still at my Post

One of the challenges of moving to America from the Philippines was finding someone trustworthy enough to watch one's existing house or property. Immediate family members were usually the first choice, followed by more distant relatives, and then trusted friends who would then either watch over or even occupy the house until the owners returned.

Leaving a house seemingly unoccupied would surely invite thieves to pillage it, or squatters to occupy it and then later refuse to leave. Worse yet, conniving relatives might be tempted to procure the house for themselves behind the owners' backs.

Ellen and her siblings were already living in America when their house in the province was burglarized. When a relative caretaker arrived there after a torrential rainstorm, he found the property literally picked clean. Its protective metal-grilled doors were hacked open with an axe, and all its valuables—down to the towels and linen—were taken away. The only items that remained were old rugs and scattered garbage that lined the floor.

According to neighbors, the theft must've occurred during a rainstorm that lasted three days. No one saw anything unusual, because they all stayed inside during the inclement weather.

When Ellen was notified of the burglary, she immediately told her caretaker to call the police, and then to take pictures. She then told him that once the investigation was finished he should clean and repair the now-empty house and remove whatever trace of the robbery was left.

Six months later, Ellen and her sister arrived from America and returned to their pillaged house in the barrio. They immediately went upstairs and opened all the drawers to see if anything remained.

Much to their surprise, a single red and green kimono sat folded in one of the drawers, still wrapped in plastic. It originally belonged to her deceased brother, and was normally tucked in-between other articles of clothing.

Ellen stared at it and stood bewildered. Why, among all the items stolen, did this particular garment remain untouched?

As a firm believer in omens and signs from the afterlife, she con-
cluded that was a sign from her deceased brother, telling her that
despite of what happened, he was still looking after her.

Vigil

Farmers were usually the earliest risers in the barrio, heading to the
rice fields to begin their work even before sunrise. They were a
common sight in front of Gloria's house, passing by individually or
in small groups before heading off into the distance. They were a
friendly and amicable people, simple worker folk of the land who
knew little else beyond their occupation, but they were quite good
at what they did.

When Gloria struck up a conversation with a farmer as he was
heading back home in the hot afternoon, she was quite surprised
when he described to her what he and the others saw while passing
by her house in the wee morning hours.

"We always see two people sitting in front of the gate facing your
house," said the old man with a wide, broken-toothed smile. His
dark complexion gave away the number of years he had practiced
his occupation. "They were an old couple."

Gloria was initially surprised, because the house directly in front
of hers was empty. Who could they be? But she later realized who
these mysterious people may have been: her deceased parents.

Her parents died when she was quite young, and despite all the
painful adversity that she and her siblings experienced while growing up, they always seemed to miraculously survive. Through all
their setbacks and obstacles, they all prospered as adults.

Gloria felt glad upon this realization. Even after death, her parents continued to look after their children. And she had no doubt
that even as she and her siblings would grow old and pass away
themselves, they would in turn do the very same thing for those who
continued to live on.

Family Ties that Bind

It was billed as a massive three-day event, the first family reunion of its kind for a clan that had never called all its members together into a single sitting. Descended from nine brothers and sisters who lived in the early 20th century, families from the United States returned to the Philippines and joined their existing relatives in the province to celebrate their historical lineage.

The festivities included a lunch in a resort that overlooked an extinct volcano in the middle of a lake, a grand picnic in the open-air rice fields, and even a parade and flower offering to the Virgin Mary inside the town's central Baroque-style church.

A videographer was hired to record the event, as was a photographer to take a massive group shot of over a hundred descendants from at least three generations.

Unfortunately, one elderly family member couldn't attend, because she had slipped into a coma while in the hospital. Grandmother Tess was unconscious and far away in Manila when the reunion took place, which made her comments all the more curious when she woke up several weeks later and spoke about the picnic in full detail.

She told her visiting sister that, during the time of her unconsciousness, she was actually at the picnic herself with the others. She eerily began recounting specific details about the event and about the relatives who attended, particulars that only someone who was actually there would know.

"I was waving to you, but you couldn't see me," she said with disappointment. "I was so hungry, because I walked a very long distance to get to the picnic." She even noted that one of their relatives was wearing a cast after suffering a broken leg.

Grandmother Tess passed away several days later. When still alive, she kept personal items and effects of her departed siblings inside a large cabinet that was located inside her room on the second floor of her sister's house. Upon her passing, her sister began giving away or disposing of the items that had been collected over the years: old clothes, wallets and purses, important documents, even uncashed checks.

But that was when Grandmother Tess was said to make her presence known again. During the wake, her sister and her sister's nieces spent the night inside Grandmother Tess's room. According to the young nieces, they heard unusual knocking coming from the cabinet that contained the collected items. They also described mysterious scratching sounds emanating from beneath the grandmother's adjacent bed.

Even when they were downstairs, the family members could feel and hear a presence on the second floor above them, from Grandmother Tess's room itself. A screen door that was normally secured open in the kitchen kept slamming itself shut when no one was around.

The house's occupants became understandably nervous about spending the night there, going as far as wearing red clothing while sleeping. This practice stems from the folk belief that wearing red prevents a departed relative from visiting the living, possibly because red was the hue of hellfire.

They speculated that Grandmother Tess's spirit was unhappy at the decision to give the sentimental items away so soon after her passing.

PART TWO

Black-Out Tales
from the City

The Fifth Floor

Norman, Jerry, and Renato were classmates in the second grade, on a campus that boasted classes from kindergarten all the way up to college in a single compound. They were more acquaintances than friends, routinely waiting on the second floor with their parents for their elder siblings to get out of class. While this free time normally afforded them innocent time to play with toys, it occasionally meant sneaking out to the outside hallway and spitting on the school guards patrolling downstairs. It was innocent fun, and ducking away to get out of view was easy enough.

It was common knowledge that the top-most floor of the five-story elementary school building was haunted, rumored to have no electricity and possessing a single coffin with a body. At night, the fifth floor was said to be particularly eerie, its windows remaining unlit. Feeding off each other's dares, it didn't take long for the three to decide to go upstairs and visit the forbidden floor.

The University of Santo Tomas, established in 1611, is the oldest existing university in the Philippines—predating even America's Harvard University.

"We'll run up as fast as we can," said Norman, "non-stop until we reach the top."

Jerry and Renato nodded in agreement, and all three stood at the base of the second floor stairwell. Given the consistent architecture of the building, all the floors were identical in appearance, and it was easy to mistake one floor for the other. This trip was just a matter of sprinting upstairs in a continuous spiral to see what was truly there.

With a signal, the three began stomping up the steps, snaking around people descending down and screaming as they got higher. They finally reached the fourth floor, and quickly noticed how dim the lights were around them. Just as they were about to enter the final dark stairwell that ascended to the legendary fifth floor, maniacal laughter suddenly erupted around them.

Without pausing, the children screamed in terror and quickly went back down the steps. They caught their breaths on the second floor, exactly where they started, and away from their parents' eyes.

"Could it have been someone playing a trick on us?" asked Jerry to his friends, panting.

"But there was no one there!" argued Norman. "We didn't see anybody."

The three friends vowed never to visit the forbidden top floor ever again.

Take it Easy

Religious statues abound in virtually all Catholic churches in the Philippines. Many are found behind the main altar, towering over the pulpit in compartments that overlook the congregation. Others stand near the entrance, greeting parishioners as they enter, while some loom above kneeling stands and are flanked with candles meant for lighting and prayer. On grand religious occasions, many statues are even carried on processions through cities and towns for the faithful to view.

Mr. Tan had the unique occupation of fixing these statues, patching them in spots, and even carving or hammering them down in others. One day he was summoned to do work on the venerated Black Nazarene, a life-size statue of Jesus bearing a leaning cross on his

Saint statues are commonplace in virtually all Catholic churches.

shoulder, which was kept inside the Quiapo Church in Manila. The sculpture's particularly dark complexion was attributed to a fire that supposedly engulfed the original galleon that transported it to the Philippines from Mexico.

Mr. Tan was hired to repair some warped wood located on the back of the statue. He was to chip away at some burnt bits and replace them with new wood.

His tools in hand, he began his repairs in earnest. Of Chinese descent and not Catholic himself, he wasn't swayed by the mystique or the adoration that surrounded the sculpture. He also didn't pay attention to the strength of his pounding, or how much it echoed in the great hall.

"Poco, poco," said a voice mysteriously, which meant, "Take it easy," in Spanish. Startled, he looked around and saw he was alone.

He continued to pound, digging and chipping away at the wood behind the statue.

"Poco, poco!" insisted the same voice, more distinct but still seemingly from out of nowhere. Mr. Tan paused once more and found no one in sight. "Who's there?" he asked, frustrated with this distraction.

He resumed his work, this time with even more determination. He didn't care how holy this statue was—he just wanted to finish the job uninterrupted.

Mr. Tan then casually glanced up to look at the top of the statue, and he suddenly froze in place.

With its body turned fully at the torso, the Black Nazarene was staring directly at him.

"Poco, poco!" it demanded sternly.

The Lower Floors

"Never ride the elevator by yourself, especially in the basement."

Students at a famous Catholic university in Manila were always admonished with that warning, in regards to a particular medical building on campus.

Local belief held that a headless nun was haunting the elevator as it reached the lower or basement levels. It would appear beside passengers if they dared to venture alone, wearing her nun's veil, but with no face or head.

This spirit was rumored to have come about from an actual incident. One day, a man was delivering several heavy plastic palettes of soda bottles on a portable dolly to an elevator.

As the doors opened, he casually wheeled the dolly inside, not realizing that there was no car there. The doors somehow had opened prior to the car's arrival.

The palettes of heavy soda plunged down the elevator shaft, crashing through the ceiling of the elevator car below and killing a nun riding inside.

Her head was crushed, and she was summarily decapitated.

This spirit now roams the lower floors, appearing next to unwary riders as they descend to the lower floors. Only the foolish didn't heed the warnings, finding themselves next to a veiled, headless passenger.

Me and My Shadow

Nardo always enjoyed being the class clown. He basked in all the attention by telling jokes to his friends, acting the fool, and even thumbing his nose at tradition. In short, he was doing things others would never get away with, and they were drawn to him because of it.

One night, he and several playmates huddled around a candle in the dark. A city-wide power blackout had all but shut his district down, and making-up games was the only thing left to do to pass the time.

They all told stories for a while, but when the flicker of their shadows against the candlelight caught their fancy, they began making shadow puppets with their hands on the nearby wall.

"This is an eagle," Nardo said, clasping his thumbs together and fanning out his fingers. His friends then imitated his gesture with their own.

"And this is a snake," he continued, curling his middle finger for the pointer finger and opening out his thumb.

His friends clapped and showered him with laughter and attention—except for one child, who didn't find his behavior amusing.

"You shouldn't do that," said Manny, a neighborhood acquaintance. "They say you shouldn't play with your shadow, or something bad will happen."

"What are you talking about?" Nardo rebutted. "I can do whatever I want."

But Manny was unmoving. "The old people say it's bad to play with your shadow, because someone might get angry and you will die."

"Who's going to get angry?" he replied with a smile. "Our grandparents? The shadows? You're dumb if you believe in those old superstitions."

He continued his antics well into the night, until the electricity finally came on and the children disbanded to go home.

Nardo casually strolled down his block, and noticed his shadow stretching ahead of him beneath the bright streetlights that towered above. This immediately reminded him of his earlier behavior, and it caused him to smile. He would have to do that again very soon.

But as he came closer to his house, he stared at his own shadow again—and noticed it didn't have a head anymore.

He gasped, and didn't know what it meant.

The following day, Nardo was found dead in his home.

On blackout nights, his friends never dared to play with their own shadows ever again.

The Clothes Stay On

Anyone who has ever stayed in the tropics for long can tell you how hot and sweltering the summer nights can be. Many of the older classrooms and dormitories didn't have the luxury of air conditioners back in the 1950s and '60s, and given the conservative attitude of most religious institutions back then, sleeping solely in one's undergarments was taboo.

But a student named Marisol decided to chance getting caught by the nuns, unable to tolerate the night heat any longer and decided to wear only her underwear beneath the sheets. But in this particular all-women's dormitory in Manila, there were rumors that the spirit of a deceased nun haunted the building, still enforcing the strict dress code and making sure all the students were abiding by the rules.

Unable to brave the heat any longer, Marisol slipped out of her conservative shirt and shorts and went under the covers in only her undergarments. At least it made the night a bit more bearable, and none would be the wiser.

But when she woke up the following morning, she was in shock when she removed the covers off her body, and found she was fully clothed.

Lesson Learned

Never underestimate the mischief that children can get into when their parents aren't home. It was near sunset when siblings Mark, Tessie, and Sandy, antsy for something to do, decided to stage a mock haunting.

The plan was for Tessie and Sandy to come running out of the house in full view of neighbors and passersby, acting hysterically at seeing a ghost supposedly inside their house. Mark was to dress up in a sheet and hold a candle to his face, appearing on the family's second-story window for everyone in the street to see.

It was simple and straightforward, definitely something that will grab attention. After a bit of planning, the three made sure that there were people walking across the road on their block before going into action.

With the house lights off against the dark evening sky, Tessie and Sandy came running out from their front gate and into the street, flagging people down to show them the ghost that was "haunting" their home. An eerie figure appeared from behind a window on the second floor, glowing like an apparition that looked ominously back.

Day or night, local neighborhoods teem with life and stories.

Stunned passersby stopped and pointed, unable to explain exactly what they were seeing. A concerned American bicyclist even stopped and took off his glasses to stare.

But with Tessie and Sandy looking on, the glow emanating from the figure suddenly got flung backwards. The siblings immediately knew something had gone wrong.

Convincing the small crowd that they were going back in, the two entered the front gate and went to the main door. Mark came running out and met them, still dressed in his sheets, but without the candle.

"I heard something behind me," he said nervously, staring at the upstairs window. "There was a sound, and I didn't know what it was. I got out of there fast!"

He didn't want to tempt fate, he later said, fearful that it could've been an actual ghost teaching the three not to fool around with the supernatural. The three later went up to the second story room where Mark was pretending to be a ghost, and saw nothing out of the ordinary. Luckily, the discarded candle didn't start a fire.

It was years before their parents found out about the incident, which the three kept quiet about until adulthood.

Playfully Yours

Edward and his four siblings all slept together in the same room at night, on the second floor in their house in Manila. It was a simple layout; two beds pushed together that were flanked by a black-and-white television set on one side and a towering detached closet on the other. With the lights turned off, the room was nearly pitch-black, with only a crack of the hallway light seeping through the door sill and an oscillating fan to keep them company.

It wasn't unusual to wake up in the middle of the night, particularly due to the stifling heat of the tropics. But on one particular night, Edward opened his eyes and saw something mysterious sitting on the top of the closet.

It was a little boy, dressed in 1920s clothing, sitting on the edge above him and dangling his feet. It was smiling and laughing.

Edward stared back in disbelief. He had never seen a ghost in the house before. He closed his eyes and began praying, hoping the spirit would leave with the power of his faith.

He opened his eyes, and saw the boy was still there.

He pressed his eyes shut and continued to pray. When he opened them again, the little boy had vanished.

Edward would later learn that he wasn't the only one who saw the ghost. His mother had seen the same spirit child on a different occasion, wearing shorts and kicking his feet while sitting on the detached closet.

A Drink in the Dark

It was customary for the maid to leave a pitcher of water and several drinking cups on a tray inside Madelle's and her brothers' room. At different times of the night, each would routinely get up and take a drink when they got thirsty. Their bedroom door was always left half-open, allowing the hallway light to illuminate the entrance, just enough to guide the children to see the tray of water.

Madelle found herself awake one night, alternately switching her eyes from the dim ceiling to the doorway. She then saw a dark silhouette standing in front of the drinking tray by the door, pouring itself a cup of water, then lifting it high to take a drink. She didn't think anything of it; the figure had curly hair like her older brother, so she figured it was just him being thirsty.

But she quickly became frightened when the silhouette suddenly vanished in place.

She covered her eyes and promptly pulled the blanket over her head in fear.

Madelle told her family of her encounter the following day, and it turned out her older brother also saw the same ghost, but at a different time.

Except he saw her taking a drink of water before vanishing.

Just Outside the Door

Bong and Rhea lived on an American military base in the northern province of Pampanga. The two met while he was serving his tour of duty in the Philippines, and she was a local worker employed at the base. They later married and began living together.

Bong was awakened by his wife one night at the sound of commotion outside their bedroom door. He immediately sat up and grabbed a weapon, listening intently to determine what exactly was happening outside. Footsteps came and went in front of their door, as if someone was pacing back and forth to see if anyone was inside their room. The noises began to shift around and intensify, occurring all around them at different walls. As the incident progressed, the clamor became more violent, sounding as if dishes and glass were falling to the ground and shattering to pieces.

The couple noticed a car circling their block outside, its headlights glaring into their room. They immediately thought they were being robbed, and that this mysterious car was being used to haul their belongings away. Fearing for their lives, Bong placed Rhea inside their closet while he waited outside to protect her.

The commotion continued for hours. Rhea would later leave the closet to join her husband, and they huddled in one corner and began to pray. They stayed in the same spot, well into morning.

The author's grandmother's house was the site of many spectral occurrences.

When the noises finally stopped at sunrise, the couple got up and cautiously left their bedroom to inspect the damages. They were shocked at what they saw outside.

Everything in the living room—and all the rooms—were safe and intact, as if nothing had touched them. And there was nothing shattered on the floor or on the walls.

A neighbor later told the couple that it must've been the spirit of a previous occupant who died in the house. It was the anniversary of this death, and he just wanted to make his presence known so he wouldn't be forgotten.

Midnight Run

Taxi cabs are essential in the big city, particularly for long distances that go beyond a tricycle or jeepney ride, and if one has heavy items or luggage to carry. A common sight around airports, hotels, and tourist areas, they unfortunately have garnered a questionable reputation for gouging unwary passengers and foreigners for higher fares.

Maricel was working late one night, leaving her office well after closing, and hoping to come home for some well-deserved rest. She immediately hailed a cab upon exiting her building, waving her hand at the first ride she saw coming up the street.

The cab slowly pulled up to the curb, and she promptly took her seat inside. Giving him her address, she immediately decompressed and began to relax.

"I can't tell you how long a day it's been," she said with a smile. "What a day."

The taxi cab driver remained quiet and kept his eyes on the road. It was late in the evening, and except for the meter display lighting the dashboard, the entire cabin was dark.

Maricel thought nothing of it at first. She was familiar with the surroundings scrolling outside her window, so she knew she wasn't being kidnapped. This particular driver just wasn't the talkative type.

"You been doing this long?" she persisted. She needed to break the monotony of the long trip back. "What's it like driving people around all day? What time do you sleep?"

Filipino culture is a blend of East and West, of history and of modernity.

But the taxi cab driver remained quiet in place. From where she was sitting, unless he turned his head to look behind him, she couldn't see his face completely.

She finally arrived at her home. Maricel extended her hand with the payment, but the man lifted his cupped hand behind him to accept without turning. Glancing at the driver's rearview mirror, she noticed that the man seemingly had cotton taped across his eyes. Was he a partially-blind driver?

Maricel retrieved a pen and quickly wrote down the driver's name and the cab's identifying numbers listed on his exposed I.D. card, which was situated just above the meter. She wanted to report him for acting so suspiciously.

The following day, she called the taxi cab company and spoke to the main dispatcher. After telling him the cab and the driver's information, she sat in disbelief at what the dispatcher then told her.

It turned out that the taxi cab she rode in the night before had been in an accident two days prior. It crashed, and its driver was killed.

Limbo Children

Edwin sighed the moment he cleared the checkpoint entrance of the military airbase. It was already late at night, and he had a suitcase of work he still needed to review sitting on the passenger seat next to him.

He was new to the base, somewhat unfamiliar with the route back to his billet housing. When he took an unfortunate turn up the wrong street, he quickly found himself disoriented amid the dim houses.

Edwin drove up one particular street and saw several children standing on the street corner.

"Excuse me," he said, lowering the passenger-side window to talk to the nearest boy. "Can you tell me where Fairfield Street is?"

The child stared back at him with a curious, blank look. He then gave him what seemingly were easy directions to get back to the main road.

"Thanks a lot," said Edwin with gratitude. But prior to driving away, he placed his hand on the seat next to him, and quickly discovered that his briefcase was missing.

He rubbed his hand on and beneath the seat cushion, as well as the backseat of his car. The briefcase was mysteriously nowhere to be found.

Edwin drove away in frustration, following the directions the boy had given him and hoping to still find his briefcase safely in his car under the brightly-lit driveway.

But the longer he drove, the more confused he became. He lost all orientation of the streets, seemingly going in circles and almost riding around in a stupor.

After what felt like an eternity, he found himself in the same street corner where he got lost before, but with the children gone. He suddenly came upon the realization that he was actually familiar with this area, and that he wasn't too far from his home.

Glancing at the seat next to him, he saw his briefcase sitting in its place, as if it had been there the whole time.

Edwin quickly drove home, both relieved and unsettled about what had just happened.

The Grotto's Pet

Much like in the United States, many Filipinos keep dogs as beloved pets. Since most families cannot afford expensive commercial dog food from the grocery stores, these pets are often fed the leftovers of every meal.

Jason had owned a dog for several years, a scruffy mutt that joyfully kept him company after he came home from elementary school. It was his best friend, a companion he would even talk to when he was having problems.

So it was extremely sad when he found his favorite dog dead in the backyard, having expired from natural causes. Rigor had set in, as did the ants.

Since his family lived across the street from a vast undeveloped field forested with tall grass, his father decided to bury the dog's body just inside the field's perimeter. Retrieving an empty rice sack, they placed the dog inside and solemnly buried it in the gloomy late afternoon.

The family had a small cave grotto that contained a statue of the Virgin Mary. It sat above a small fishpond that flanked the house's garden, which itself was situated just inside the front gate. The dog would often use this side grotto as a platform to leap over the property's barb-wire fence to get to the street and bathe in the passing cows' manure.

When the family finally returned to the house after burying the dog, Jason's siblings noticed that the statue of the Virgin Mary had

At its heart, Filipino culture revolves around agriculture.

turned on its pedestal inside the grotto. It was tilted forward against the cave wall, leaning in the direction of the dog's grave across the street.

A Shimmer above the Water

Ghostly nuns and priests are commonplace in native folklore, particularly in historically religious schools and hospitals. One all-women's school in Manila was rumored to have a haunted koi pond.

This pond was situated next to a covered walkway, and was surrounded by picnic tables. It was an area frequented by students regularly. Containing a grotto, this pool of water also had the distinction of being a dumping ground of sorts: students regularly dropped their bits of refuse into the water.

But it also had a more grim reputation, particularly at night. The koi pond was said to be the haunt of faceless nuns that sang under the full moon. People reported seeing these apparitions in full view around the pond, but despite being in close proximity to them, the nuns' voices sounded as if they were far away.

Head of the Class

The death of a fellow student can be hard on a student body, particularly if the student was popular. One such girl suddenly passed away one day, expiring from an enlarged heart. The school administrators of the high school decided to honor her memory by planting a tree in her name. But for some reason, the campus still felt uneasy about her death, and any memorials attached to her name.

During the 1970s, class lessons sometimes came in audio form. Students would spend time in what was called a Speech Lab, where they would wear headphones and listen to stories or lectures electronically.

One night, the school's janitor entered the Speech Lab to clean it after hours. The room itself was in a slope, its rows of seats descending down to the teacher's desk like in a stadium. He began his routine of sweeping the floors and wiping the desktops, starting from the top and then going down the steps.

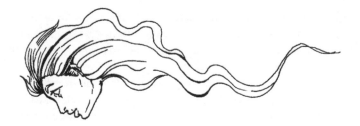

As he was cleaning, he just happened to glance at the teacher's desk below.

He saw the disembodied head of the dead student, eerily floating back and forth above the desk.

The Tightening

Speech Lab, where high school students listened to audio stories and lectures in 1970s, wasn't generally known to be haunted.

But this assumption changed one day when a class of students used the facility. Listening to their lessons, one student suddenly noticed her classmate was crying.

When she came over to help, her friend motioned that she was unable to pry to headphones off. It was squeezing her head tighter and tighter.

A teacher arrived and tried to help. After a few minutes, the headphones suddenly loosened from the girl's head. No one could explain why they tightened in the first place.

Pitch Black

Marites and several of her friends were invited for drinks after work one night, by a public relations man who owned a club that had undergone several incarnations. Currently a popular hang-out place among the early 20s crowd, this establishment was previously an upscale restaurant, and even a risqué burlesque bar notorious for showcasing low-brow female entertainment.

When the club's floorshow had wrapped up around midnight, Marites and the public relations man went upstairs to his office so she could use the restroom (it is known as the "comfort room," or "CR" in the Philippines). Finding the restroom on his floor out of order, they both then proceeded to use the one on the club's main floor.

The public relations man escorted Marites to the ladies' restroom, as he needed to use the men's room, as well.

She had just finished relieving herself when, before she could even sit up, the lights of the restroom suddenly went dark. Closing her eyes so as not to strain them, she dressed and left the stall, groping her way to the direction of the door. Closing and opening her eyes in the pitch blackness, she then noticed light seeping in between the bottom of the door and floor.

Keeping her back to the restroom's tiled wall so she wouldn't stumble over anything, she continued to inch forward until she was

The Spanish colonial influence can still be seen in historical architecture, as in this archway in Intramuros, Manila's famous walled city.

able to exit the room. To her surprise, the entire floor outside the restroom was fully lit.

Seeing a nearby security guard making the rounds, Marites quickly motioned for him to come over to tell him what happened.

"Why did the lights in the women's comfort room go out?" she protested.

"But ma'am, they're not out," he answered back.

"Why don't you go inside and check?" she insisted.

He entered the room, then came back out. "The lights are on."

The public relations man came out and asked what the fuss was about. Marites told him the story and insisted that she wasn't making a fuss over nothing, and that the lights did indeed turn off when she was using it.

It was already past midnight, and she needed to go home. She dropped the matter and joined her other friends. Still curious about the incident, the public relations man asked her if she saw anything unusual while inside the restroom.

"I couldn't see anything because it was so dark," Marites responded, still irritated. "I didn't let my eyes wander because I was just so focused on finding the direction to the exit."

"You're lucky you didn't see anything," he said ominously.

Marites would later learn that a woman had committed suicide inside that particular restroom, and that there had been many reports of a mysterious white aura appearing to late-night users in the dark.

Do as We Say...

Of all the children that attended this elementary school, Roger was the only one who had the unfortunate habit of spitting. He spat whenever he could, particularly in front of his classmates. He even took glee in doing it, defying the teachers and the parents that complained.

"You should stop doing that disgusting habit," his elders admonished. "One of these days, something bad is going to happen to you if you don't."

But young Roger persisted.

One day, on a cloudy afternoon that was on the verge of a downpour, he decided to stay after school and climb up a coconut tree.

"Come on inside," his classmates said. "It's about to rain."

"I'm going to do whatever I want," Roger said proudly. "No one is going to tell me what to do."

As he crawled up the tree and found himself several meters above the ground, a lightning bolt suddenly shot down from the clouds and struck him in the head.

His head as obliterated, and all that was left of him was a decapitated body hugging the trunk.

His teachers found him the next day, and they quickly admonished the children from spitting.

"That is what happens, children," one teacher said, "when someone does something that they're not supposed to."

The children quickly took this lesson to heart.

The Painting

The dormitory in this all-women's college was very old fashioned, its sleeping quarters almost barracks-style, with each student sleeping in individual bunks. Hanging on the second floor was a painting of a woman in a village scene holding a basket. It was a rather large picture, situated above the doorway next to the exit.

There were persistent rumors in the school that the woman in the picture actually stared back at people. It was also common knowledge that, when everyone got called downstairs for dinner at 6 P.M. after praying the Angelus, no one should stay behind alone in the second-floor sleeping quarters. "Unusual" events were known to occur when the place was empty of students.

Lori was so into her homework one early evening that she decided not to go downstairs to have dinner with her classmates. She sat at a desk that students regularly used to study, situated at the end of the room and surrounded with chairs. The painting hung above the doorway next to her, by the exit.

Continuing her work, she suddenly got hungry and began rummaging through her belongings to find food.

As she casually looked up at the painting above her, she noticed that the woman in it had disappeared.

When she turned to her left, she saw the same woman standing right next her, with a horrific, evil stare.

Lori screamed and immediately ran out the room. When she turned around to look behind her, the woman from the painting actually began following her.

Lori sprinted down the steps and ended up at the refectory, in hysterics.

Faculty members and students later went upstairs to investigate what had happened, and saw the woman who had supposedly chased Lori was back inside the painting.

The large painting was eventually removed and was rumored to have been stored inside a cloister.

Wḩat a Steal

Roman and Manuel couldn't believe the bargain they procured for themselves and a family of relatives. The two managed to rent out a magnificent old-style hacienda in the tourist city of Baguio, nearly impossible to achieve at such a low rate and at the height of the season.

But problems surfaced immediately the first night they stayed at the property. The children that accompanied them began crying, saying that they kept seeing an old man around. Lights throughout the house began to flicker, and the sound of footsteps accompanied by chains was present all around them.

Roman and Manuel shared a room away from the family. The following night, however, the two slept in different quarters, with Roman in the bedroom and Manuel on the sofa. Roman was suddenly awakened by a knocking on his door. It was Manuel, frightened out of his wits, describing the sound of footsteps and chains dragging around the sofa where he slept.

Manuel later calmed down, and decided to try the sofa again. He returned to Roman's bedroom not fifteen minutes later, still describing the footsteps and the chains, but this time it was circling directly around where he slept.

The two men and their relatives had had enough. The next day, Roman and Manuel left the family behind in the house while they traveled on foot to summon a cab some distance away. When they came back with the ride, the family was surprisingly huddled in front of the property. They described how the lights of the top and bottom floors began to flicker out of control. And when they left the hacienda out of fear, the gate behind them rattled uncontrollably.

They loaded their luggage into the cab and left the hacienda immediately, now knowing why the property came at such a bargain.

When a Push comes to...

Valerie stood inside her living room and stared out into the balcony that faced the street. Her children had been playing in the front yard for most of the day, so she decided to call them in for some much-needed rest.

She just happened to glance behind her, and saw that the door to the playroom was slowly closing by itself.

A disembodied hand suddenly appeared between the swinging door and the doorframe, as if it was the one pushing it shut. Even after the door was fully closed, the hand continued to float in place.

"Oh God," Valerie blurted out. "What's happening?"

She looked at the door again, and saw that the hand had mysteriously vanished.

Her mother-in-law occasionally spent time in the living room, but Valerie was all alone when it happened.

She was so spooked that she immediately called a monsignor friend that night.

Hearing her story, he calmed her down and suggested she could've been just tired. Her eyes and her mind may have been playing tricks on her. To this day, however, Valerie still doesn't know what she really saw.

Visitation Rights

Jun was a student at a prestigious local high school in his teens. His family lived on the second floor of a two-story apartment that was also adjacent to his relatives' house situated literally next door. In fact, this house was actually his father's original home growing up, along with his aunts and uncles.

But after his father passed away, Jun later moved in with these same relatives and called that old house home.

One night, as he arrived from school, Jun unexpectedly saw a mysterious ball of light drifting from his old apartment and down to his relatives' home next door.

With the house unoccupied that particular evening, he followed it inside in the dark, watching it float past the living room and up the stairs, only to disappear into the room where his father used to stay when he was a boy.

Jun thought it may have been his deceased father just paying him a visit.

Inheritance

Flor was always curious about her past. She was particularly fascinated about the lives of her grandparents, of how they lived and what it must've been like to exist in the early 20th century. Her family was also seemingly never without ghost stories, or tales of the supernatural. It wasn't until she asked her mother about her family tree did she finally realize why this was so.

These experiences apparently ran very deep in her bloodline.

Flor learned that her maternal *lola*—her grandmother—was originally from Aklan, a region in the central Philippines that was notorious for witchcraft. She was extremely religious, but also superstitious, very knowledgeable in the so-called "old ways."

Her *lola* was said to have possessed the dried tail of a stingray, which she used to counter bad spirits and black magic. She would whip the mysterious black pigs that entered her living room to make them disappear. She also used it to strike that mysterious last step of the stairwell in their old house, the one that would bulge or expand mysteriously.

She even kept a bottle of oil, which she claimed would start boiling when a sorcerer or witch was nearby.

The grandmother also had a unique method of procuring numbers when playing the local lottery, called "jueteng." Getting the egg sac of a native spider, she would then paste it under the bottom of a drinking glass. Holding it against the light, she would stare at the shapes and patterns created to get her numbers.

Sometimes she won, and sometimes she lost.

Hark the Herald

Amir's mother had just picked him and his siblings up from elementary school when he first heard the sounds at home.

It was a typical hot afternoon in Manila; ice cream vendors, pushing their wheeled carts, would normally pace the streets outside his house, clanging their hand-held bells to signal their arrival.

But this time, all Amir could hear were the family dogs howling. They wailed eerily for several long minutes, seemingly for no reason and much to the surprise of his family.

Amir then walked outside to the front balcony, and saw a man walking up the road towards their house. When this man began knocking on the front gates, he immediately summoned his mother to see who it was. "There's someone in front!" he said, running back inside the house.

It turned out to be his uncle who had traveled far from their father's province, announcing the news that his grandfather had just passed away.

That night, they left for the province to attend the wake. Amir and his family unexpectedly had to go through several military checkpoints on the way to his grandfather's house.

It turned out to be the first day the Ferdinand Marcos government imposed Martial Law upon the country.

Stand by Me

Derrick was playing alone with his tricycle in the driveway one morning. Bored with just riding around in circles, he came up with a new game of slamming his ride against the house's front iron gates to create a loud sound.

Accelerating towards the gates, he would then turn the steering wheel sharply to one side, causing the tricycle to spin around, the rear tires slamming flush against the metal panel. The impact almost sounded like thunder.

He tried it twice, and found it quite enjoyable.

But on the third attempt, he suddenly found himself sprawled on the cement just before the tricycle slammed into the iron gates.

Something had grabbed him snuggly by his armpits and lifted him off the seat, causing him to land safely on the ground on his back.

Brushing himself off quickly, he stood up and looked around to see who may have saved him.

But Derrick was alone in the driveway. He re-enacted his actions slowly, going as far as gently falling to the ground to see if he could've just fallen on his own. But there was no way he could've landed on his back from the angle of his turn.

That was when he started believing in guardian angels. He couldn't help but wonder what would've happened if he wasn't tossed from the tricycle on the third try.

Just Checking Up

Abigail woke up in the second-story bedroom one morning, and found herself alone. It had been several days since the funeral of her older brother, who had just died from an enlarged heart.

She normally slept with her older sister, but when she noticed she wasn't beside her, Abigail deduced that she must've gone downstairs for some coffee.

The Manila Cathedral near Intramuros.

It had been a tiring stretch of days for the entire family.

Still **half-asleep** and laying on her right side, Abigail casually turned over to her left. That was when she saw her deceased older brother standing at the foot of her bed, smiling and dressed in his usual trubenized outfit. She smiled back instinctively without pause and turned fully over.

She then realized who she just saw. "Why is he there?" she asked herself with her eyes closed. "He's dead."

She quickly ran down the stairs in a panic and told her family.

Abigail marveled at how clearly he appeared to her. They were extremely close when he was alive, and she wondered later if it was just her memory of him from the funeral that she actually saw standing at the foot of her bed.

Only the Wind

After a quick one-week stay in the Philippines to attend her mother's funeral, Gemma was finally ready to go back to the United States. She and her sister Cristine had just spent most of the day at the Philippine Embassy, to make sure all her papers were in order.

Arriving home at night, all they wanted to do was relax. With Cristine opting to stay downstairs and watch the television, Gemma decided to go upstairs and make sure her passport was secure and readily handy. When traveling between both countries, it was the most important document to have for identification.

But as soon as she climbed up to the second floor, she suddenly couldn't find the passport anywhere. A mysterious scent then began to permeate the air around her. It was the sweet smell of azucena, native flowers used decoratively in wakes and burials. As she began to get overwhelmed, Gemma quickly ran downstairs and told her sister what happened.

She trembled in place as Cristine held her to calm her down. Worse yet, she couldn't find her passport upstairs.

Their sister Jessica, a teacher, then came home from her classes. "What are you guys doing down here?" she asked with concern.

"Come with me upstairs," insisted Gemma, making sure her elder sister went up first. "Help me look for my passport. By the way, do you wear perfume?"

"No," said Jessica. "Never."

When they arrived, the scent had disappeared. "There's no smell here," reassured Jessica.

Gemma then found her passport, exactly where she had left it before.

In a Blink

Whether it was herself or the maid, Jocelyn made sure someone kept an eye over her children while they slept in the master bedroom upstairs. They were never to be left alone.

This room was one of the cooler places in the house, complete with nice linen, a big oscillating fan, and a balcony that faced out into the street.

Wanting to go downstairs to relax, Jocelyn called the maid to take her place upstairs. As she came down and reclined on the sofa, she then saw a figure descend the steps from the master bedroom upstairs.

"Oh, you left the children," she said quickly, wondering why the maid left her post.

But a voice suddenly spoke out beside her. "But ma'am," said her maid, "I haven't gone upstairs yet."

Jocelyn stared at her in disbelief. "But I just saw you come down. Haven't you gone up already?"

"No, ma'am," said the maid innocently. "I was still in the kitchen cooking."

Jocelyn was dead sure the person she saw descend the stairs was the maid. She then recounted the rumors that her oldest sister told her about the plot of land their house was built on. During the Japanese occupation in World War II, it was believed to have been a cemetery. Filipinos who were pointed out by native spies as collaborators were summarily executed and buried there.

Visiting Hours

When Grandmother Teresa suffered a stroke while living in the province, her relatives decided to move her to the city where she could be better taken care of. Staying at her granddaughter's house,

she would've had more relatives to look after her, plus easier access to a city hospital in case of a medical emergency.

A person was even assigned to look after her, a Mr. Gus. He was a retired army sergeant who doubled as a driver to Grandmother Teresa's son-in-law.

Mr. Gus kept vigil outside of the grandmother's room one night. He sat just across the entrance, which was an open wooden door protected by a closed screen door that allowed the breeze to come in.

He had always fancied himself as a "sensitive," someone who was attuned to the supernatural. As he sat at his post that particular night, he saw three people dressed in white suddenly materialize and walk through the front screen door without opening it. One was a woman with a shawl over her head, another was a tall man with white hair, and the third was a short man, also with white hair.

From their appearance, Mr. Gus assumed that they were the grandmother's relatives and husband, arriving to take her away.

He began to weep. "Please don't take her," he implored them. "It's not her time yet."

He waited for a while. Everything felt like a dream to him, but he knew he was wide awake.

A few moments later, the three apparitions eerily exited the room through the same screen door, again without opening it, and disappeared.

Mr. Gus was relieved when Grandmother Teresa didn't die. He felt his plea was heard.

Neither Here nor There

As a disc jockey for a local radio station, Ed had pretty much heard everything under the sun. He'd been fielding calls from the public for years, hosting a radio show with his signature booming voice in the city of Pampanga on popular topics that spanned the Filipino experience. From politics to celebrity gossip, public injustice to sports, even tragedies and triumphs, he had been at the forefront of announcing issues to a loyal audience.

Exchanging ghost stories is a very popular pastime in the Philippines, and while Halloween is normally an occasion celebrated in America at the end of October, it also coincides with the somber All Saints Day (*Todos Los Santos*) and All Souls Day (*Todos Los Difuntos*) holidays. The two-day event is meant to venerate one's ancestors, prompting thousands to flock to their local cemeteries to maintain their deceased's gravesite.

While dressing up in costume and going trick-or-treating from house to house may not be a Filipino pastime (save, perhaps, for the wealthy, or the Americans living in military bases), locals indirectly observe it by swapping stories of the supernatural.

On one particular Halloween night, Ed fielded a call from a listener that really wasn't any different from the others that were previously phoned in. The only constant was that all the storytellers were convinced that what they were relaying was true.

"Something visited my daughter during the last black out, while she was asleep in our living room," said an American who was living in Manila. "It was a tall, dark man, with large red eyes."

Ed was a little surprised; it wasn't too common for Americans to call his radio show.

"And it had this... big, sharp nose," the man continued, "like the beak of a bird. He just stood there and stared at my daughter before disappearing."

"Thank you for the call," said Ed politely, moving on and continuing to field other uncanny stories. In a culture rich with supernatural characters, it was just another tale to entertain his audience's obsession with the unknown.

But on the nights that followed, he continued to receive calls on his show, from different listeners throughout the region who described the same eerie, beaked figure visiting their homes and scaring their families.

It appeared that Ed had dismissed the story far too quickly than it deserved.

Wait 'til your Father gets home

When Rosalie and her family first learned that their dad had passed away in the hospital, they immediately left their house to be by his side, leaving only their housemaid and houseboy to look after their property. There were many details that needed to be attended to, so after a tiring night of bringing their father's body to the funeral parlor and then settling all other peripheral issues, the weary family finally came home after midnight.

But much to their surprise, they saw their house fully-lit, and their caretakers wide awake.

"Is your father really dead?" the two asked curiously upon meeting.

"Of course he is," Rosalie's mother replied. "We just came back from the hospital and the funeral parlor." She couldn't believe how absurd this all sounded.

"But we just saw him here," said the houseboy ominously. He recounted how they saw her father standing at the front door of the house, just prior to their arrival. "I asked him if he was supposed to be dead, and he turned around, walked away, then vanished just as the car pulled up."

The caretakers immediately turned all the lights on to search for the man, but found no one in sight.

Actually, Rosalie and her family weren't afraid of the incident at all. They didn't even consider their father to be a ghost haunting their house, but rather as the same man they loved who was just visiting his home and his family.

They looked forward to his visiting them again, but he never reappeared.

A View from the Trenches

As a nurse in a modern hospital in Manila, Josephine had heard her share of stories that bordered on the supernatural. Her outlook was a unique balance between science and the Catholic faith, where cultural beliefs could sometimes clash with the rules of physics and biology. But as a trained professional, she managed to exist and flourish in both realities, and was able to view them objectively while being true to herself.

"I don't know what the word 'ghost' means," she said. "When I was a kid, I associated ghosts with something scary. But as a grown-up, I believe that persons who just died usually do the things they normally do, until such time they realize that they are already dead."

Despite working in a place where deaths often occurred, she insisted that she had never directly experienced anything supernatural. "I am not one of those who has a third eye, people who can see paranormal occurrences."

But ghost stories were also a constant while she was growing up. "During high school, a teacher in Spanish class who was also a school administrator would pass by a convenience store to buy bread and coffee before class started at 7 A.M. He passed away one morning, but people in the convenience store, including a classmate, saw him in the store as if buying the same coffee and bread. "For a high school student, that's something scary that we call *nagmumulto*, or the ghost of the teacher coming back."

Despite her objectivity, Josephine was also well-aware of the various beliefs and eccentricities that her colleagues and her patients were exposed to where she worked.

"Hospital personnel could sometimes see figures of persons walking at night in hallways or at different units of hospitals, even when they were sure that no one else was there. There were times when those who are really afraid would just ask a colleague to accompany them during their tour of duty, especially if they were going to a place where no one was around."

She also heard stories of patients' conditions getting worse during confinement because of the presence of ghosts. There were medical personnel who did not want their patients to be brought to a particular room, because of the presence of ghosts or spirits. "Maybe this is similar to the cases when dying persons see dead people roaming around. I do not know if this is the same as the stories of elders who say that the dying person will be met by dead people."

There was even a belief that the spirits of dead persons came and fetched those who were dying. "We hear a lot about persons who are sick seeing their dead relatives and calling their names. My dad was hospitalized for three days before he passed away. He was awake, but on respirator during those days. He communicated through writing, and he wrote the names of his grandmother and some dead relatives on paper while pointing to something we couldn't see."

Josephine continues to balance her faith with her nursing, and despite all that she's heard, she maintains she still hasn't experienced anything supernatural firsthand. "I don't know if I believe it; I just know that I am always just too tired to experience spirits roaming in hallways or rooms."

PART THREE

Hauntings on American Soil

When you Wish upon a Sign

James pressed his face firmly against the window every time their car passed by the store on the way to the mall. He couldn't see much past the huge sign that hung over its entrance and dark-tinted windows, but he didn't really need to. All that really mattered was that the store was called "Japanese Imports."

And in his mind, that meant imported toys.

He had been an avid collector of Japanese action figures and models for several years, characters that were shown on a local television station in the afternoon. Most of these items, however, were only sold at the coast a hundred miles away, making "Japanese Imports" all the more intriguing. Could it be that a local toy store had set up shop in his town, a new place where he could indulge his imagination aside from the neighborhood comic book store?

But seeing this store only in passing finally took its toll. It was always closed on the late afternoons and weekends when they drove down that particular route, so the only way to find out what was the store's inventory was to actually call and ask.

On a Sunday evening, James pulled out the area phone book and looked up the store's listing and number. He promptly called it and waited with anticipation, not even considering if the store was closed at night.

When a voice answered, his twelve-year old eyes widened. "I... was wondering what kind of toys you have?"

He began inquiring about the store's toy products, listing names and descriptions of his favorite Japanese super-heroes. To his delight, the man said "yes" to all his inquiries. "We have the one with the horns, and the woman," he answered. "We have a bin of these figures."

"Thank you very much!" said James, smiling as he hung up. He now knew of a place where he could buy the entire collection of his beloved action figures.

Realizing he still had more questions, he called the store back a few minutes later, but was answered by a different voice.

"Ummm... I just spoke to a man about the toys you had," he said. "I wanted to know if you had these other characters, too..."

The man on the phone sounded older, with a slight Japanese accent. "I'm just the night watchman here," he said, sounding as if he was in the middle of doing his rounds. "But yeah, it looks like we have what you're looking for. You need to come in for yourself and see what we have."

"Thank you!" repeated James. His second call reaffirmed what the first man had said. He even told his mom about his conversation with the store. Sometime soon, he was going to have to persuade his dad to bring him to the store to shop.

When he came home from school the following afternoon, James still had more questions for the store's workers. He called Japanese Imports back, but was greeted by yet another person.

"Hello," answered a woman politely.

"Ummm… I called last night about some toys you guys have, and I talked to two men."

"Sir," she said with concern, "we're closed on the weekends, and no one was here last night."

James paused, unsure of what to say. He could hear a lot of commotion and conversation behind her. "But I spoke to a night watchman and he described to me your toys."

"We don't have a night watchman," she responded. "We don't sell toys. We're an auto-parts store."

James retrieved the phone book and made sure and it was very same number from the previous night. He called it again and heard the same woman, immediately hanging up upon hearing her voice.

Whenever he passed by the same store into his adult years, he still couldn't explain whom it was he spoke to, and why they said the things they said.

Colors that Run in the Dark

Despite transferring to a four-year university from a community college, Eddie still wanted to finish his two-year degree from his previous school. That meant taking classes while on summer break from his university studies. Deciding to become an art major early on, he thought it would be beneficial to have two college degrees in his resume for future employment.

Luckily, the only elective class available that was related to his major was a water-coloring class, one of his favorite hobbies.

Throughout the short summer semester, James and his class-mates spent their time inside their classroom painting fruit, or outside in the quads illustrating landscapes. But he wasn't quite sure how to grasp the next locale where his instructor said they were supposed to meet for next week's session. They were to convene at the neighborhood cemetery.

The class arrived at the historical Broadway location in the early afternoon. Aside from a handful of busy groundskeepers, the sprawling area was almost empty. The students felt quite uneasy, as most of them had never been inside one for any amount of time, and they couldn't get past its stigma of death.

"This is a great place to paint," said his instructor. "Pick a spot and paint it on your canvass."

The class dispersed and fanned out in all directions. This particular cemetery was historical, said to contain major American political figures that dated back to the Civil War. The closer one got to its center, the older the graves became. Many of the tombstones listed the dates and method by which the person expired, and unfortunately, many of them were children.

But the cemetery was also surprisingly peaceful, cool in temperature compared to the summer heat beyond its gates. James even saw rare birds perched among the treetops.

"I'm sorry, but I can't do this," said a classmate, fearful of her surroundings. She wavered on whether or not to stay, ultimately deciding to pack-up her clipboard and paints and drive away.

James walked around a bit longer before picking a spot and beginning to paint. It was a simple, tree-lined walkway, nothing too elaborate. He didn't want to illustrate any specific tombstones, from fear of somehow drawing its essence to himself.

His Filipino heritage made him more superstitious than the average person.

He painted for a little over an hour, chatting with his classmates and comparing impressions. He actually thought this would be a great place to have a picnic. He left much earlier than the class's three-hour term; since they were offsite and his instructor was nowhere to be seen, he thought he could probably get away with it.

James went home to his mother's house and immediately changed his clothes. One of his family's superstitions was that one should always change one's clothing right after attending a wake or a funeral, to prevent its essence of death from clinging to one's body.

He thought of little else that evening. His eventful day at the cemetery was over, and all that really mattered was watching TV and then sleeping.

He laid on the floor at the foot of his parents' bed, watching a show while everyone else was outside in the living room. There was a dresser next to him that was capped by a large mirror that reflected the wall to his left.

As James was watching his program, he casually glanced at the mirror looming above him to the right. That was when he saw a dark silhouette reflected on it. It was in the shape of a man.

He quickly turned his head to see who it was. This wasn't his eyes playing tricks on him; he had seen mirage glimpses from the corner of his eyes before in the past, but they were usually just flotsam that followed the turning of his head and eyeballs. James stared at this silhouette for a full second before it flitted away from the mirror.

He cautiously stood up and looked behind him. The only place this figure could've gone to was the adjacent bathroom at the rear of the room. Grabbing a stick, he cautiously searched the back, and found no one.

He couldn't help but wonder if something had followed him home from art class that night.

A Brush with the Unknown

It had already been a curious week for Kate. While waiting to go to volleyball practice at her high school several days earlier, she casually took off her backpack and placed it on the floor. With her back facing the wall, she suddenly felt a commotion from behind, as if someone was tugging firmly on the belt loops of her jeans. But there was nobody behind her.

She told her mom about the curious incident, then thought nothing else of it for the rest of the week.

Several days later, Kate was half-asleep on one particular school night, sharing the bedroom at home with the rest of her four siblings. Her eldest brother lay in his own bed just adjacent to hers, while the remaining three slept in a bunk bed that was located across the room.

All was peaceful, and even the room lights were left on.

Kate suddenly felt someone gently touch the back of her head. She lay in place and smiled, expecting to see either her mom or her dad looking over her as she turned over. But to her surprise, there was nobody there.

She sat up and looked around her bed, checking to see where her hair may have gotten snagged to produce that sensation.

That was when she felt a scrubbing sensation against her scalp, as if someone was vigorously mussing the hair behind her head.

Kate screamed at the top of her lungs and ran out of the room. Awakened, her siblings sprang from their beds and ran after her, wondering frantically what she was running from.

Her eldest brother, a martial artist who practiced the Filipino stick-fighting art of Arnis, retrieved his bamboo stick and flung it at Kate's bed before leaving, hoping to strike whatever it was that scared her.

A Requiem for Two

There were two women who were in a relationship. Unfortunately, the union soon ended when one of them, a nurse, decided to leave and move out of the house they were sharing. In her grief, the rejected woman began stalking her ex-partner over the next few weeks. One early afternoon, when the nurse returned to their old home to pick up some clothes, the rejected woman blocked her car in the driveway with her own vehicle, then shot and killed her with a handgun. The rejected woman took her own life afterwards, in a murder-suicide.

When news of the nurse's death reached her workplace, her co-workers at the hospital were shocked. The deceased nurse's shift was from 3:00 P.M. to midnight, and on the very same day she expired, her colleagues swore they saw her going about her usual routine of walking the hallways, going in and out of the elevator, and even getting food from the employee lounge.

How could she have possibly died that day?

Friends then began feeling the deceased nurse's presence in their homes, places where the deceased had frequented while still alive. One woman even claimed to have seen the nurse's apparition in her third-floor apartment, subtly peeking down through the curtains in-between gentle flutters. It frightened her so much that she didn't even want to sleep in her own apartment alone, for fear of encountering the deceased unexpectedly.

But in the end, the tense situation had seemingly resolved itself. One of their friends had a dream months later where all three were seated around a table on a bright sunny day. The deceased women apologized to this friend for all the trouble they caused, and stated that everything was alright now.

Flotsam in my Mind's Eye

While a teenager, Erica once worked as a waitress in sprawling, multi-story retirement home for the elderly in downtown. One late afternoon, she needed to go to the utility room in the basement downstairs to retrieve aprons, as well as get a can of her beloved snack, a grape soda drink.

Upon exiting the elevator and walking towards the room directly across the hallway, she immediately saw a figure walking towards her from the left.

"Is that you, Carl?" she asked, immediately recognizing this person as a fellow co-worker. "It's me, Erica. I'm down here getting some aprons." She made it a point to announce herself so there was no mistaking who was present on the basement floor.

She retrieved the aprons and got her soda from the vending machine that was located just inside the door.

But when she turned around and headed back to the elevator, the person she saw walking towards her had disappeared. The hallway that led directly to the utility room was completely empty. She didn't even hear any footsteps on the nearby stairs of a person leaving, nor the elevator in front of her making a sound to go back upstairs.

Erica quickly returned to the main floor. She later learned that the person whom she thought she saw in the basement wasn't even working that day.

Left or Right?

Gail stopped at the intersection as she drove off the freeway exit, unsure of which way to turn. She had finished eating dinner with a friend earlier in the evening, and was now traveling on work-related business to a distant county several hours from her hometown.

All that was left to do was check in to her hotel and call it a night for tomorrow's scheduled presentation. Unfortunately, she was also lost.

She decided to turn right at the stop sign, seeing some lights in that direction before exiting the freeway, and hoping to find the next main road to get her bearings. But as she continued down the road, the path grew darker and darker, and she now wondered if she somehow made a wrong turn along the way.

Arriving at a bend in the road, she decided to double-back and try the other direction. She stopped her car and maneuvered a three-point turn, starting and stopping in angles until she was able to fully turn around.

To her horror, her headlights suddenly panned across a landscape of tombstones. She somehow found herself on the immediate outskirts of a cemetery.

Gail planted her foot on the gas pedal and screeched out of the area, going in the opposite direction and eventually finding her hotel.

She checked in and headed to her room. With her laptop, projector, garment bag, and business suit in hand, she fumbled for her key card and opened the door, using her shoulder to brace the door open while she hauled her luggage in through the door. That was when she saw something from the corner of her eye.

She had always made it a point to position herself away from danger, so she was constantly aware of her surroundings. When she saw a figure coming towards her, she didn't want to take the chance of encountering anyone alone while in the hallway. She hurriedly heaved her gear inside and began shutting the door.

But before the door could close, she suddenly saw a shadow of a person traveling across the wall before her. She was fully expecting to see a person walking across her doorway just behind it... but there was no one.

The shadow appeared and vanished, but with no one casting it against the light.

After a few moments, Gail peeked out into the hallway, and saw no one. She kept her door shut and locked the rest of the evening.

Through the Eyes of Babes

It was Christmas Eve, and Miguel and his two-year old son were busy getting ready to leave for his mother-in-law's house. His wife Marie was already there, leaving earlier in the day to help prepare the traditional *Noche Buena* dinner for the rest of the family. It was a quiet, uneventful evening, and all that was left to do was to eat, and then hide his son's presents so they could later inform him that Santa had dropped them off at the stroke of midnight.

This was a tradition his wife Marie and her siblings had grown up with, and she wanted to maintain it in her own family as well.

While Miguel was shaving in the bathroom, he suddenly heard the sound of laughter coming from the hallway. Curious, he peaked outside and saw his son ecstatic with joy, running and playing up and down the corridor.

"I am happy," his son said. "Nana's here."

"Who are you playing with?" asked Miguel. They were the only two people in the house.

"Nana," repeated his son. "She's playing with me."

"Nana" was their term of endearment for Miguel's mother, who had passed away before his son was even born. Although his son had never met his grandmother, Miguel kept his mother's picture on display in the living room.

Miguel wasn't the least bit scared. His mother was the most loving person he had ever known, and he realized that she must've just been visiting her grandson for Christmas.

But that wasn't the last time the son would see his deceased grandmother. On another occasion, the couple had just left their in-laws' house after a party. While Marie buckled herself inside the car, Miguel went around and secured their son in the baby seat behind her.

The couple then saw their child staring intently out the window above him.

"What's wrong?" asked Miguel. "What are you looking at?"

"Nana," said his son.

This time, the couple looked at each other and became nervous. "Where is she?" asked Marie.

Her son raised his hand and pointed, his gaze and gesture slowly going from his nearby window, down to the front hood of their car.

But that was the last time their son claimed to have seen his deceased grandmother.

Hide and Shriek

After a long, tiring day at the office and a visit to the grocery store, Janet finally came home to rest. Eight months pregnant, she walked up the stairs and joined her husband Bobby in their second-story bedroom. He had made it home prior to her arriving.

But, needing to retrieve something from the linen closet downstairs, she soon headed back down. The couple intentionally kept the overhead lights turned off when the kitchen and living room were not in use, so she needed to flip the light-switch on to see in the dim hallway that led to the closet. Three bedrooms flanked this linen closet, one positioned to the side of it, and the other two across the walkway in opposite diagonals.

Just as she turned the lights on, a dark silhouette suddenly emerged from the adjacent bedroom while its door was still closed. It crossed the narrow hallway right in front of her, then entered the nearest bedroom across the linen closet, again with the door still closed.

Janet screamed and ran up the stairs in three literal bounds, pounding on the door and crying out, "Bobby, there's somebody downstairs!"

Her husband quickly retrieved his rifle without hesitation, tucked a pistol in his waistband, and began heading downstairs. But Janet quickly stopped him in place; what if what she saw wasn't actually a ghost, but a burglar?

"Let's just call 911," she insisted, opting to play it safe.

The author's old home in Quezon City, rumored to be the site of executions during World War II. Demolished in the 1990s, a new building now stands in its place.

Contacting the police, the couple was given instructions on how to allow the officers access to their home while remaining safe in the second floor. Through a series of signals, they ultimately gave them their house keys via the balcony that overlooked the backyard.

When the police came in and checked the house thoroughly, they found the bottom floor completely empty.

While supernatural occurrences weren't common in their household, there were other instances where its occupants felt a mysterious presence while alone. Unexplainable footsteps and creaking had been heard from the second floor, and occasional glimpses of passing figures in the hallways were also noted.

APPENDIX:

List of Supernatural-related Terms

Ada. Term for a native fairy.

Agimat (adimat, adjimat). Type of protective amulet, talismanic stone or gem
that grants its bearer various supernatural powers and abilities. It is kept
inside one's pocket or worn as a pendant. Synonymous with anting-anting
(see entry).

Aklan. Province on the island of Panay in the Western Visayas region
of the Philippines. Bordering the equally infamous province of Capiz,
it is reputed to be the home of the dreaded aswang (see entry).

Al-allia. Ilocano. Native term for a ghost.

Amamanhig (Amalanhig). Capiz. The corpse of a deceased person
who refuses to die until it tends to its unfinished business incurred
when still alive. Only then can this restless spirit find peace. These
issues can range from paying off immense debt, to having proper
funerary rites.

Angel statues. Cement statues of angels, used as architectural
decoration in office buildings and museums, sometimes believed to
come to life at night and walk around. Their footprints have been
seen on the sand garden that acted as the sculptural base.

Anghel. Derived from Spanish; term to describe a Christian angel.

Anino. Tagalog. Term for a shadow, sometimes referring to a ghost.

Anito. Term to describe spirits that are the object of worship, sometimes referenced as idols, nature spirits, and even ancestor spirits.
The term is said to be derived from the Sanskrit "hantu," meaning
"the dead."

Aniyani. Pangasinan. Native term for a ghost or spirit.

Anting-anting. Umbrella term for a diverse class of talismans or amulets worn as protection against evil spirits, as well as to gain mystical powers and attributes. The more common are small medallions that can be bought from sidewalk vendors near Quiapo Church in Manila, depicting Catholic religious images such as the

Holy Trinity, Christ, angels, and the Virgin Mary. The more exotic types come from objects in the natural world, ranging from seeds, odd stones, unusual roots and herbs, various preserved body parts, and even fetuses.

These talismans are obtained by inheritance (passed from one bearer to another), or by defeating supernatural demons who safeguard them. They are popularly believed to emerge from the heart of a banana plant at midnight, and the bearer must fight guardian demons to prove his worthiness.

Depending on the type, they give the bearer various attributes, including invisibility, great strength, invulnerability from cuts and bullets, elusiveness from capture, and even wealth. There are various incantations to maintain the anting-anting's power, as well as tests to prove its effectiveness.

Aswang. Umbrella term for a diverse class of shape-shifting witches and demons found throughout the country. Linguistically, the term is said to be derived from "keswange" from the Moluccan archipelago, relating to the suangi witch. Another source says it comes from the term "asuasuan," which means having the likeness of a dog.

By day, people who are aswangs are anti-social or reclusive, possessing no philtrum between their nose and upper lip. Staring into their eyes meant seeing one's own image, but reflected upside-down. But at night, they turn into creatures who can either walk or fly, and are fond of devouring livers, unborn children in the womb, or fresh corpses. Some are known to turn into dogs or enormous black pigs, while other types replace bodies they've stolen with banana trunks.

There are several ways by which a person can become an aswang: biological inheritance through one's parents; through contamination, eating food tainted by the creature; or have the influence transfer from an aswang to a living person just prior to the creature's demise. The absorbing of matter that evolves into a bird-like creature inside the victim's body is also another way.

Folklorist Maximo D. Ramos classifies them into five types: shape-shifting weredogs, blood-drinking vampires, self-segmenting viscera suckers, malevolent witches, and corpse-devouring ghouls.

The classic weapon used in defense against them is the tail of a stingray.

Ataul. Term for coffin. See also kabaong.

Balete tree. Ficus benjamina. Native species of banyan tree widely believed to be the home of various supernatural entities, including ghosts, towering kapres, and diminutive duwendes.

Bangungot. "Nightmare," from the root words bangon (to rise) and ungol (to moan). Phenomena where a person dies from his nightmares if he is unable to wake up. Occurring when sleeping immediately after a heavy meal, this condition affects almost strictly middle-aged Filipino males. It was first reported in medical journals in 1917.

Bangkay. Tagalog. Term for a corpse or dead body.

Bantay. Term for a person's guardian spirit.

Bari bari apo. Ilocano. "Please move aside." Phrase used when passing or stepping over anthills or mounds on a path, meant as a sign of respect to the dwarves believed to be residing inside. Offending them or desecrating these homes mean incurring retribution. See also tabi po.

Beheaded priests. Apparitions seen occasionally in churches and religious schools, clergymen said to have been executed during Spanish colonial times and the Japanese occupation during World War II. Appearing at night individually or in groups, they are described as a headless and dressed in robes.

Whether in the city or the province, Catholicism permeates all of daily life.

Bolang apoy. Ball of fire. See santilmo.

Bowing trees. Common motif in supernatural folklore, where a person traveling in a secluded road or area suddenly encounters trees (often towering bamboo) that mysteriously lower their branches to the ground, as if barring his way.

Bulul. Ifugao. Wooden carving of a seated human figure, representing one of forty granary deities invoked in various harvest rituals.

Commonly depicted in pairs, these male and female statues appear regularly as decorative motifs in grain containers, spoons and walking sticks, at times standing and even dancing.

Buntot pagi. The tail of a stingray, the classic native weapon used against evil spirits and witchcraft. It is sometimes used to strike an afflicted victim to drive away occupying spirits.

Capiz. Province on the island of Panay in the Western Visayas region of the Philippines. Bordering the equally infamous province of Aklan, it is reputed to be the home of the dreaded aswang (see entry).

CCP Ghosts. Popular urban folklore surrounding the Cultural Center of the Philippines' Manila Film Center building. During its construction in 1981, scaffolding supporting workers reportedly collapsed, sending on unspecified number of men plunging to the quick-drying cement below. Instead of aiding the victims and retrieving the mired bodies, officials were ordered to keep them in place, pouring over them for the sake of meeting the construction deadline. Since the building's completion, patrons have reported seeing mysterious shadows and hearing disembodied voices from the walls, presumably caused by restless spirits believed to still be entombed inside the cement.

Cementerio. Term for a cemetery.

Cemeteries are curiously vertical in the province.

Crucifix. Catholic symbol representing the death of Jesus Christ, either worn as a pendant talisman or hung on the wall to protect against evil spirits.

Demonyo. Derived from Spanish; term to describe the Christian devil, or generically a demon.

Diablo. Derived from Spanish; term to describe the Christian devil, or generically a demon.

Diwata. Native term for divinity or godhead, derived from the Sanskrit devata.

Duwende (duende). Derived from Spanish, meaning "dwarf." It is described as an old, dark-complexioned man that only measures between 1½ to 2 feet in height, said to reside inside ant mounds or underground. Wearing a cap (which comes in different colors, depending on the regions) and occasionally a beard, it is sometimes considered beneficial to people and children if befriended, but is notorious if offended. People who come across its ant mound home in the glade must first ask permission to pass (see "tabi po" and "bari bari po" entries), for failure to do so might incur a curse for punishment, particularly those that desecrate its home.

Engkanto (enkantada, ingkanto). Derived from the Spanish "encantado," meaning enchanted or bewitched. Term to describe magical, fair-skinned beings said to reside in beautiful mansions, palaces, and even cities, although to the human eye, their domiciles appear as balete trees (see entry) or large boulders. They are capricious, attractive spirits, extremely wealthy and known for playing tricks on mortals, occasionally courting them, and even kidnapping children into their world. They dislike loud noises, and eat lavish foods, but without salt.

It is due to their unpredictable nature that they are greatly feared, not knowing their disposition when encountered inadvertently. They can cause illness, which only a sorcerer can cure. They are known regionally under different names: tamawo (tumawo), banwaanon, tiaw, meno, tagbanua, and Ti Mamanua. They are often referred to by Visayans as "dili ingon nato," or "people not like us." The three most famous engkantos in folk belief are Mariang Makiling, Mariang Sinukan, and Maria Cacao.

Espiritista (spiritista). Derived from Spanish; term to describe a spirit medium.

Espiritu. Derived from Spanish; generic term to describe a spirit or a soul.

Faith healing. Umbrella term for different systems of folk healing that use unconventional methods in diagnosing and treating various illnesses. Depending on the practitioner, it combines the use of herbs, native massage, prayers (see orasyon), communicating with helpful spirits, and the invocation of Catholic saints. The most controversial form of faith healing is the so-called psychic surgery (see entry).

At the foot of the Manila Cathedral, established in 1581.

Gabi ng Lagim. Extremely popular radio play about native stories of horror and the supernatural. It ran for several decades, and has even been made into movies.

Guni-guni. Generic term that refers to the imagination, or to something unreal. It's usually in reference to the supernatural.

Halimaw (halimao). Generic term for an evil spirit, monster, or supernatural entity.

Hantorah. Special solution made of roots, herbs, and oil kept in a small bottle. Prepared by a supernatural specialist, it is used to detect the presence of aswangs (see entry) and other supernatural entities, bubbling and overflowing when in close proximity.

Hospital apparitions. The ghosts of doctors and nurses, seen in elevators, hallways, and wards, going about their former routine as if still alive. Encountered at night, they are sometimes described as floating and without feet.

Ibiris. Tausug. Malevolent spirit that has been compared to the Christian devil, considered the source of all human sin and misdeeds. Its sole purpose is to entice people into committing evil deeds. Present in all human beings, his influence can be denied by sheer determination.

Ilang-ilang. Native flowering tree whose fragrant blossoms are said to be the favorite of malignos or evil spirits.

Impakto. Generic term to describe malevolent fiend, ghost, or demon.

Impiyerno. Term for the Christian hell.

Japanese Soldier apparitions. Common ghost seen at sites occupied or frequented by Japanese soldiers during World War II. Most appear going about their previous routine, as if still alive.

Jin islam. Tausug. "Moslem spirits." Diverse class of spirits said to follow the commandments of God.

Jin kapil. Tausug. "Non-believer spirits." Diverse class of spirits who do not follow the commandments of God, said to occasionally bring about sickness in people.

Kabaong. Term for a coffin. See also ataul.

Kakarma. Ilocano. Term for a ghost.

Kalag. Visayan. Native term for a human soul, but often referencing a ghost.

Kaluluwa. Tagalog. Term for the human soul.

Kapre. Derived from Spanish "cafre" that references Muslim infidels, which itself is derived from the Arabic "kafir." A towering, dark-skinned giant said to reside in balete trees (see entry), it scares passersby while smoking its trademark enormous tobacco cigarette that smolders in the dark. It is also known to have the power to change into various animals.

Kulam. Generic term for sorcery or witchcraft. A practitioner is a mangkukulam (see entry).

Kutob. Literally "heartbeat." However, it can also mean having an ominous premonition.

Lamang lupa. Term to describe so-called "spirits beneath the earth," entities that dwell underground that can cause illness to those that offend them.

Langit. Tagalog term for the Christian heaven.

Maligno. Generic term for an evil spirit or entity that prowls the night.

Malik-mata. Term to describe seeing something that wasn't really there, or mistaking something for something else.

Mamaw. Generic term for a frightening ghost or spirit, sometimes referenced to scare children.

Mananambal. Cebuano. Term to describe a native folk healer, shaman, or even sorcerer. With the use of prayers, incantations, herbs, and sacred oils, these male and female practitioners cure victims who are afflicted with supernaturally-derived illnesses. They are also said to enlist the aid of various spirits to determine the cause of affliction.

Manghuhula. Tagalog. Term for a fortune-teller.

Mangkukulam. Generic term to describe a witch or sorcerer that uses various means to attack its victims with debilitating hexes and curses (pricking dolls, etc.). Often solitary, anti-social old women living on the outskirts of town, they were described by early colonial Spaniards as "emitting a fire that could not be extinguished."

Manlalabas. Term to describe a ghost or spirit that shows itself to people.

Mantianak. Spirit of a child that was buried with its deceased mother. It waits for unsuspecting victims and attacks as they pass by. It has also been described as a baby possessing a long beard, said to turn itself into a human being. If its wails can be heard loudly, it is said to be far away. It its wails are dim, it means it is close by.

Mga bata ng limbo. Batangas. So-called "children of limbo," believed to be the spirits of aborted fetuses. Those who hear their wailing are said to experience headaches and insomnia, which in turn makes them pray for these lost souls to reach heaven.

Mt. Banahaw. Located on the island of Luzon, on the southeast region of Quezon Province. Rising to an elevation of 7,100 feet, it is considered by locals to be a holy site, a center of powerful psychic energy that's believed to be the home of spirits. Various religious sects, hermits, and healers utilize its shrines, trails, caves and purifying waterfalls for worship and communing with nature.

Mt. Cristobal. Located on the island of Luzon, on the southeast region of Quezon Province. Unlike its neighbor Mt. Banahaw (venerated by devotees, see entry), this mountain is considered its polar opposite, often labeled "devil's mountain" for its negative energies and evil spirits.

Multo. Derived from the Spanish word "muerto." Tagalog term to describe a ghost or a spirit of the deceased.

Mumu (mumo). Generic term for frightening spirit or entity, usually used in the context of scaring children from going out alone at night.

Mutya. Type of talismanic stone or gem that grants its bearer various supernatural powers and abilities. Those who seek to obtain it from a banana blossom at midnight must fight off the demons that guard it. Synonymous with anting-anting (see entry).

Nabati. Tagalog. To have been greeted by a ghost, which in turn can develop into illness.

Nakablaawan. Ilocano. "Being greeted." Illness derived from being greeted or touched by the ghost of a dead relative.

Nakalbit. Tagalog. To have literally been tapped or touched by a ghost, sometimes resulting in the area of contact to become dark blue in color.

Nakatuwaan. Term to describe to have been amused with by a ghost.

Naluganan. Ilocano. Native term for spirit possession.

Nangliligaw. Spectral children said to cause drivers who ask them for directions to get lost from their destination, disorienting them into driving in the same wayward route repeatedly.

Napadlaawan. Ilocano. Experiencing an unexplainable cold feeling when around the presence of a spirit, often in the context of premonitions of a relative's death.

Napaglaruan. Term to describe to have been played or toyed with by a ghost.

Nasasahaon. Type of spirit possession, described as being subjugated by an evil spirit that inflicts illness upon its host body.

Nun spirits. Ghosts of deceased Catholic nuns, common in religious all-women colleges. They have appeared in various guises, sometimes faceless or beheaded, and at times even playing musical instruments in a group at night. Some are notoriously conservative, mysteriously dressing dormitory students who sleep only in their underwear during hot, humid nights.

Nuno sa punso. "Old man of the woods." Dwarf-like entity similar to a duwende (see entry), said to wear a farmer's gourd hat and resides in anthills, underground or in secluded areas. Diminutive in size, it possesses large quantities of gold and occasionally interacts with people. Like the duwende, it inflicts curses on those that desecrate its earthen home. Also known as *matanda* and *taong-lupa*.

Orasyon (oracion, urasiyun). Incantations or prayers derived from Latin or Latin-sounding Filipino phrases used to cure illness, as protection against harm, to control the weather, and even deflect bullets. They are sometimes written on pieces of paper and used as protective amulets or talismans (see anting-anting).

Religious educational institutions abound throughout the country.

Oro, plata, mata. "Gold, silver, death." Numbering system applied to the steps of a staircase or a walkway. Each of the three words corresponds to a step, and local belief dictates that the total number of steps that lead to the next floor, when counted in that specific sequence of words, must not end with "mata," which means death and is considered extremely unlucky.

Padugo. Ritual blood-letting performed before the construction of a house. It involves slitting the throat of a white chicken and allowing the blood to drip around the site. Careful attention is paid to the animal's dying gestures, which can determine the site's prosperity. Varying in use from region to region, the blood is splattered about the grounds to drive off evil spirits, as well as to prevent accidents from occurring during construction.

Panaginip. Tagalog. Term for a dream that one has at night. Within the context of the afterlife, appearing in dreams is traditionally believed to be a method used by the deceased to communicate with the living, whether it's to convey a message, project good or dire premonitions, or simply say hello and make its presence felt.

A popular folk belief is that if a person dreams that his teeth are falling out, someone in his family will die.

Pangontra. Counter-measure, usually in reference to canceling out or neutralizing bad luck, illness, or sorcery.

Pantasma. Derived from Spanish; generic term for a ghost or spirit.

Pantom. Derived from Spanish; generic term for a ghost or spirit.

Patianak. Regional term synonymous with the dreaded tiyanak (see entry).

Pausok. Type of house fumigation and purification using smoke, meant to drive away evil spirits.

Psychic surgery. Controversial method of surgery performed by faith healers, using their bare hands to literally enter an afflicted patient's body without the use of a scalpel or anesthesia, and removing organic matter and even foreign objects that are believed to be the source of illness. The faith healer will then withdraw his hands, clean the area, and show that there are no wounds or scarring.

Skeptics, however, say that the method is a fraud, claiming that the faith healers use sleight-of-hand techniques in producing the retrieved matter, palming small packets of blood and chicken entrails in their hands and producing them when needed.

Pugot. Term to describe someone who has been beheaded. Several native ghosts appear in this manner.

Robinson's Mall creature. Manila. Extremely popular urban legend during the 1980s. The wealthy owner of a mall chain was said to have sired a son who was half-man, half-snake. This hybrid was rumored to have lived under one of the malls itself, specifically beneath the women's dressing room. A hidden trap door would send the unsuspecting victim into the creature's chamber, where she would then face its amorous advances. A popular actress reportedly encountered the creature, but was offered money if she didn't make it public. Curiously enough, the emblem of a serpent was painted in the central atrium of some of the malls.

Santilmo. Derived from "Saint Elmo's fire." Ball of fire (bolang apoy), said to be the souls of those who perished at sea. They are also believed to be the restless spirits of those who were murdered, who died by accident, or were condemned to wander the earth until their sins were expiated. They've even been known to lead people to buried treasure. Sometimes referred to as "elflight," they appear in inclement weather in swamps and fields, leading unsuspecting travelers astray.

Satanas. Term for the Christian satan.

Saytan (saitan). Maranaw, Tausug. Term for a broad class of Muslim evil spirits, said to inhabit banyan trees and rocks. They possess those that trespass into their domains without excusing themselves or entering without permission. They are also known to inhabit the bodies of dangerous animals.

Scapular. String necklace with religious Catholic imagery, worn as a talisman to protect against evil spirits.

Shake, Rattle, and Roll. The Philippines' most famous horror movie anthology from Regal Films. Traditionally playing in the theaters in December, it showcases stories of fantasy and the supernatural using both veteran and up-and-coming teen actors.

Sinakayan. Tagalog. Term to describe a person who has been possessed by an evil spirit.

Siquijor Island. Island located in the Central Visayas region of the Philippines, between the islands of Negros and Mindanao. It is reputed to be the home of various forms and practitioners of native witchcraft and sorcery.

Sirena (serena). Derived from Spanish meaning "mermaid," she is described as a beautiful, dark-haired woman from the waist up, but having a fish's tail for a torso or legs. Native mermaids live in both rivers and in the ocean. Often blamed for mysterious drownings in swimming holes and rivers, it is known to its occasionally bring people to its underwater kingdom, temporarily enabling them to breathe underwater. Some mermaids are said to require a human sacrifice once a year, and sometimes offer their captives a potentially fatal riddle, "what do you want to drink and eat?" If the captive replies "water" or "fish," then he is immediately killed, because they refer to elements related to the mermaid's environment. It is also known regionally as *kataw* and *duyong*.

Spirit Questors. The Philippines' most recognized paranormal investigative group. Originating from a college course taught by Tony Perez in Ateneo de Manila University, its members use traditional Native American techniques in communicating with spirits and non-human entities to promote unconditional love and peaceful co-existence.

Sumpa. Term for an applied mystical curse. It is also a type of protective talisman, described as the fragments of holy objects originally contained inside a church.

Tabi po. Tagalog. "Excuse me." Phrase used when passing or stepping over anthills or mounds on a path, meant as a sign of respect to the dwarves believed to be residing inside. Offending them or desecrating these homes mean incurring retribution. See also bari bari apo.

Taglugar. Visayan. "Of the place." Generic term for environmental spirits that reside within a specific area or natural objects such as trees or boulders.

Tamawo. West Visayan. Magical, fair-skinned beings said to reside in beautiful mansions, palaces, and even cities, although to the human eye, their domiciles appear as balete trees (see entry), or large boulders. See also engkanto.

Tambalan. Visayan. Term for a folk healer, medicine man, or quack doctor who specializes in curing supernatural afflictions.

Tawas. Type of supernatural folk diagnosis, where the practitioner drips a lit candle's wax into water. He then analyzes the patterns formed on the surface and determines the cause and remedy for the affliction.

Tiyanak (Tianak). Malevolent dwarf-like entity that takes the form of a wailing baby seemingly lost in the woods. When a concerned passerby attempts to pick up the child, it then assumes its true, hideous form and violently scratches the victim, or drains him of blood or life. Some accounts say that tiyanaks are actually the spirits of unbaptized children or of aborted fetuses. See also murito.

Todos Los Difuntos. All Souls Day. Catholic holiday (similar to Mexico's Día de Los Muertos) held on November 2, where relatives of the deceased would visit and clean around their loved ones' gravesites, spending the day praying and even eating within the cemetery grounds.

Todos Los Santos. All Saints Day. Catholic holiday (similar to Mexico's Día de Los Muertos) held on November 1, where relatives of the deceased would visit and clean around their loved ones' gravesites, spending the day praying and even eating within the cemetery grounds.

Tubignon. Visayan. Water spirits, whose permission must be asked if one is to bath in their waters. They are known to cause illness to bathers.

Vampira. Generic term for a male or female blood-sucking vampire.

White Lady. Famous apparition of a woman dressed in white, said to haunt Balete Drive in Quezon City. This street has an abundance of balete trees (see entry), which is traditionally considered the home

of various supernatural entities. Folklorists contend that the ghost was originally a woman who was raped by Japanese soldiers during World War II, although the term "White Lady" has evolved to describe any female apparition dressed in white that's been seen all over the country.

As most accounts surrounding her appearance come from taxi drivers and motorists, the White Lady fits the classic "Vanishing Hitchhiker" motif and its variations. She's often seen by the road-side, procuring a ride, only to mysteriously vanish in the back seat upon arriving at her destination. She has also been compared to the Mexican "La Llorona" apparition.

Yawa. Visayan. Generic term for a demon or devil, evolved in usage to refer to a non-Christian pagan.

9 780804 841597